RECKLESS
heart

RECKLESS heart

JANE SUEN

Reckless Heart

This book is a work of fiction. Names, characters, places, and incidents are products of the author's imagination or are used fictitiously. Any resemblance to actual persons, living or dead, events, or locales is coincidental.

Jane Suen books are available for order through Ingram Press Catalogues.

www.janesuen.com

Printed in the United States of America

First Printing: November 2022

Ebook ISBN: 978-1-951002-23-7

Paperback ISBN: 978-1-951002-24-4

Audiobook ISBN: 978-1-951002-25-1

To the loves in my life.

1

———

MARY SIMMONS GLANCED AT THE BRIDAL BOUQUET ON the coffee table, where she'd tossed it last night. The morning sun shined on the blush-pink and white roses, the green gum leaf, and baby's breath, all wrapped and tied with flowing, silky ribbons. She sat down on the couch, sipping her first cup of coffee. Yesterday, she'd caught her sister Katie's bouquet. Her twenty-eight-year-old younger sister had practically shoved it in her hands, shouting, "Mary!" to get her attention. It was an easy catch, meant for her and her only.

Mary had feigned surprise and delight, while her heart did a sad flop. Did anyone notice? She was still single at the ripe old age of twenty-nine. Her chin quivered at the thought of turning thirty—alone. Her eyes landed on the flowers again. She leaned in to smell the faint, sweet scent of the roses.

Katie had a beautiful New Year's Day wedding.

Mary was happy for the exuberant bride, now on her dream honeymoon with her new husband, Chase. Timmy, the kid Chase was raising after his brother Kenny and sister-in-law Darlene had died in a tragic car accident, was in the capable hands of Katie and Mary's mother, who'd moved into Katie's new home while the newlyweds were away on their trip.

Life hadn't quite turned out the way Mary wanted. Where had the time flown? In the blink of an eye, she'd be in her thirties. And what was there to look forward to in her forties? Fifties? The days seemed to march faster now, she brooded as she flipped another page on her calendar.

Startled by a shrill ringing, Mary glanced at her cell and saw it was Laurie calling. She hesitated, pulling herself together before she answered her phone.

"Hey, did I wake you?"

Mary let out a half-yawn. "Nope, but I'm still not wide awake yet. How come you're so chipper this early?"

"I'm an early riser."

"Why are you bugging *me*?"

"Well, this is my first call, now that we're related."

"We are?"

"Yes," Laurie chuckled, "since my cousin married your sister."

"Uh... so this makes you, what... my sister Katie is your cousin-in-law?" Mary mumbled.

"Right, my cousin's wife. What does that make you?"

"Darn, I need more caffeine. I can't think straight... what are we?"

"I think maybe kin of some sort. Don't ask me to explain it."

"I won't," Mary said, breaking into a laugh. "Ha! You called this morning to ask me this?"

"Actually, no," Laurie said. "I called to ask if you've had breakfast yet. Do you have plans?"

Mary sighed. Oh yeah, like she had her appointment book filled. If Laurie had asked her over a month ago, she would have answered, "Yes, Jim and I..." The words would have automatically rolled out without any effort on her part to link them together. But Jim, once her longtime boyfriend, was now her ex-boyfriend. It felt strange, a part of her life gone. Leaving his name out in conversations, returning his stuff, removing all traces of him from her place, deleting his photos from her social media where he had a presence.

"No," she said, firmly. "No plans."

"We'll go eat breakfast," Laurie said, then prodded cheerfully, "Let's go! It'll be fun. I promise."

"What about Ryan?"

Laurie laughed. "You mean, why am I leaving my husband alone?"

"Well, you're practically still newlyweds. You just got married last year."

"Ryan is a big boy. I love that he's so understanding and knows when to butt out." Laurie giggled. "Besides, he knows I'll make it up to him."

"Uh-huh, and I won't ask how. Ryan is a lucky guy." Mary laughed, knowing also what an easy-going guy he was.

"Don't I know it! Or maybe I'm the lucky one," Laurie said. "Meet you at the diner in thirty minutes, okay?"

"Sure." Mary tapped the red "end" button. The most recent calls from Jim were still logged on the call list. She took a moment to reflect. They had good memories. A few great ones. But she knew they'd reached the end long before the words were uttered, finalizing the split. Laurie was right. She needed to get out and have some fun.

2

———

MARY ARRIVED AT THE DINER RIGHT ON TIME. SHE stomped the snow off her shoes and went inside, standing at the entrance to survey the room. The dining room was in full swing with the breakfast crowd. People were laughing and talking over the clinking of glasses and tableware, and some screaming kid was throwing a tantrum, his shrill cry heard over the din as the waitresses belted out their orders and bells dinged when the food was ready. She spotted Laurie, already seated at a table, a glass of water in front of her and another one placed across the table. She made her way over, skirting coat-laden chairs in the way.

Mary had gotten to know Laurie when she served as maid of honor and Laurie was matron of honor at Katie's wedding. Laurie had cooked up this thing about having a plus one at her wedding last year, and thanks to her planning and her kind-hearted meddling, Katie and Chase became each other's plus ones then, and now they were married and on their honeymoon. Jim had served as Chase's best man, although he and Mary had broken off their relationship a month before Katie and Chase's wedding. Their split had been amicable and without hostility. Despite a lingering sadness, Mary put up a cheery, good front and kept on friendly terms with him during the big day.

Laurie looked up from the menu and caught sight of her friend, and her smile beamed in welcome across her fresh-scrubbed, makeup-free face.

"Good morning." Mary slid onto the seat and gave as cheerful a greeting as she could muster. She knew she didn't fool anyone, least of all Laurie.

"I've ordered coffee for us," Laurie said, eyes twinkling.

Mary nodded gratefully as the waitress approached with two steaming mugs of the house-brand coffee.

They ordered quickly—eggs and buttered toast for Mary, and blueberry pancakes for Laurie.

Mary grasped the warm mug with both hands and sipped the dark brew. It was bitter, and just what she needed now, what she thirsted for—not the light, flavored brand that was usually her favorite. She let out a satisfied sigh and set the mug down.

"No cream or sugar?" Laurie asked as she flicked a sugar packet, tore it open, and poured the contents into her drink.

"I like it black," Mary said. She craved the caffeine,

and drinking coffee always made her feel more alert and energetic.

The waitress returned with their order, carrying two plates of food and a bottle of syrup, and set them down on the table.

After she left, Mary took a bite of her buttered toast, crunchy on the outside, but soggy and soaked with melted butter in the center. She licked around the edges, catching clumps of sweet butter clinging to the crust in semi-solid form.

She watched as Laurie drizzled blueberry syrup over the stack of pancakes. She wondered if Laurie felt sorry for her after the split with Jim. Why did she ask her out? Mary was a big girl. She didn't want Laurie's or anyone else's pity.

"Well hello, ladies," a man's voice said.

At the sound of the rich, masculine voice, Mary froze in embarrassment, acutely aware of the butter dripping from her lips as she recognized him. She knew the handsome, dark-haired man standing at their table. He had looked amazing yesterday at Katie's wedding. Well-dressed, sophisticated, and sleek in his finely tailored suit. Today, he had on a casual, russet-tan-colored sweater and jeans, and his thick, carefully groomed hair was tousled this morning.

Mary wiped away the yellow droplet on her chin and managed a greeting. "Hi, Brad."

Laurie was smiling. "Hey, Brad, would you like to join us?"

"Sure, thanks." He pulled back a chair and took his seat, leaving enough room to stretch his long legs.

They had been in the same year in school and had been in classes together. Katie was a year younger, and for a brief period, had a crush on Brad when they were kids. Mary had seen Brad at Katie's wedding and reception, although he'd been seated at another table. The year before, he'd attended Laurie's wedding. She remembered he had asked Katie to dance with him that evening, which didn't sit well with Chase. She thought Brad hadn't come alone then; he was with another woman, a blonde she didn't recognize.

"You know Mary," Laurie said, stating the obvious, even though she knew.

"Yes, since elementary school," Brad said.

Mary felt his stare, bold and with a glint of amusement, as he directed his attention to her. The Brad she knew in school was a lanky kid, shy and sensitive. Mary slid a side glance at this gorgeous, confident man sitting at their table. She leaned over to reach for her glass of water, close enough to catch his light, manly scent. Her hand shook. *Why was she acting like a silly schoolgirl?* She hurried to take a quick sip of water, spilling a few drops over the rim.

Mary gave a polite smile. They were friends in school, had grown up together and were classmates. Did Brad remember when they were kids? The lazy, hot summer days, the silly games they played after school, the worn-out blue book bags they dutifully lugged to classes and back home, their mad dashes to the playground at recess.

"Now look at us, all grown up and almost middle-aged," Laurie said.

"Hey, speak for yourself." Mary snorted and pretended to be shocked. Laurie was her age, but she acted like a mother hen sometimes. Everybody knew that about her, and nobody minded.

The waitress showed up with a glass of water and a set of tableware for Brad. He ordered quickly—eggs, hash brown, a biscuit, and coffee.

She listened to the grown-up Brad, his voice smooth and mature like a fine bottle of wine that had aged well. He had left their small town a boy and came back a man. A real man.

"So, how long are you here this time?" Laurie was asking him, a shade of admonishment in her voice. He'd left right after her wedding last year.

"I'll be staying for one more day."

Laurie stared at him, chewing her lip. "You have plans?"

He shifted in his chair and leaned back. "I've been working on this for a while now. Something I've wanted to do." Brad raised his eyes, taking a thoughtful pause before he continued. "But I need to do it right."

"What is it?" Laurie pressed.

"A new project—a tiny home community." He paused as he made eye contact with the two women.

"You'll build it?" Mary asked. She had heard Brad was in the construction business.

"Yes, in the city where I live."

Mary couldn't help noticing that Brad's eyes sparkled, and the look on his face was intense and purposeful. It radiated energy.

"Specifics. Oh, do tell!" Laurie said.

He smiled at her and continued. "I envision a community of eco-friendly tiny homes with green space, a community garden, and..." He lifted an eyebrow. "Well, maybe walking trails, a greenhouse, and a picnic area."

"It sounds wonderful," Laurie exclaimed, clasping her hands together.

"You have a strategy?" Mary asked.

"Yes. I'll manage the budget and run the business. I've developed a plan and put together an experienced team of managers and people to bring this project to life. There's a lot of preparation involved in getting started." Brad grinned, the smile lines deepening around the corners of his eyes.

3

BRAD EYED THE PLATEFUL OF STEAMING FOOD SET IN front of him. Tender, perfectly scrambled eggs piled next to greasy hash browns. Homemade biscuits and thick pats of butter on the side. The waitress filled his mug of coffee before she left.

"Ladies?" he asked.

"Don't mind us. We ate already," Laurie said.

He put a fork in the eggs and got down to business.

Brad hadn't expected to see both women at the diner this morning. He'd had a brief conversation with Laurie at Katie's wedding, and she'd teased him about not spending enough time here when he was in town. He said he wasn't leaving right away this time. Then she talked him into breakfast and said she'd let him make it up to her. It would be almost like old times, when they'd hung out together, she had said.

It was a surprise to see Mary at breakfast. He heard about her breakup with Jim. They'd been together for so long, everyone had assumed they'd get married. He and Jim had been close years ago, before Mary.

Each time Brad received a wedding invitation, he'd wonder if it'd be Mary's turn soon. When Laurie and Ryan married last year, he remembered the wedding reception—Mary jumping out of her chair, arms outstretched to hug him in an exuberant greeting. Jim was next to her. But Brad had asked Katie to dance, as he knew she was unattached. Then Katie and Chase rekindled their relationship after they danced at Laurie's wedding, and they got married yesterday.

Laurie's phone rang, and she took the call. He guessed it was Ryan from the way she cooed and giggled.

"I've got to go." Laurie ended the call and scraped back her chair. She smiled and turned to Mary. "You'll stay here with Brad?"

"Sure," Mary said, as Laurie hurriedly pulled on her coat, snatched her purse, and left.

The waitress approached with refills for their coffee and cleared Laurie's plate at the table.

Brad was now alone with Mary and found himself suddenly timid and tongue-tied. Why was it easier when there were three of them? He had run high-stakes meetings efficiently and smoothly. He had brought his adversaries down and outwitted them. He was known for his quick wit and smart comebacks, never at a loss for words—until now, sitting next to Mary.

He peered intently into his half-full mug, studying

it like it was the most interesting thing in the world, and he could not pull his eyes away.

She broke the silence. "Are you okay?"

He raised his head and stared at her, but he didn't answer.

"You okay?"

He watched her lips move and form the question again. He cleared his throat and downed the rest of the coffee in one gulp. Then he set the mug down.

"I'm glad you're here," he blurted out without thinking.

She was smiling now, a shine in her eyes. Her face was like an open book, transparent and without guile. She wasn't playing games. He knew she heard him and responded honestly. He didn't have to guess.

He noticed her thick eyelashes, soft brown eyes, the perfectly shaped lips with a rounded cupid's bow, and her thick, chestnut-brown hair pulled back in a clip, exposing her slender neck.

He felt an urge to protect her. To keep her safe. And selfishly, to keep her away from other men. Whoa, where did that thought pop out from? Brad had never allowed himself to think this way. Maybe because she hadn't been his. He'd pushed away any hope —until now.

4

MARY COULDN'T BELIEVE HER EARS. BRAD WAS GLAD SHE was here! Her heart did a little flip. It was how he said it, in a matter-of-fact way, without making a big deal, and he made the statement with his eyes level on hers. She held his gaze and looked into his brown eyes, basking in their warmth, instinctively trusting him. This man, whom she'd known since grade school, was now sitting beside her.

Her heartbeat quickened. She repeated his words in her mind. Was she reading too much into it? People said things all the time and didn't mean it. "Let me know how things go," or "We'll talk soon," or "I'll call you." Was Brad just being polite?

They hadn't exchanged words of affection. They hadn't touched. Mary had debated whether to stay after Laurie left. She could have made an excuse and left, too. Yet she had stayed. Maybe some part of her deep inside had been curious. Maybe, just maybe, there was something more.

Brad had left town over ten years ago, and then she'd seen him a few times when he came back on occasions like weddings, but they were always brief stays. They'd led separate lives and didn't communicate. She'd heard bits and pieces about his accomplishments over the years. He wasn't the type to brag and kept himself low-key. She remembered when he'd failed at something in school, he'd try again and again until he succeeded. He was smart, persistent, and confident.

He'd also never been married. She'd wondered about that, too. Was he too busy building his business and working his way to the top? Had he dated much? Only once, at Laurie's wedding, had she seen him with someone—dancing with the blonde she'd assumed was his date.

Mary blinked. He was asking her a question. Her mind had drifted elsewhere. Had he been talking to her about his project? She hadn't been paying attention. "I'm sorry," she mumbled.

"I'd like to take you somewhere. Would you like to go now?"

"It—where is it?"

"It's not far. We can talk about the project on the way." His eyes lit up with excitement.

Oh, right, he wanted to tell her more about his project.

"Okay, let's go," she said, reaching for her things.

Brad paid the bill and helped her with her coat. His hand brushed her neck. It was the lightest touch, unintentional, but it sent a signal to her brain, a pleasurable twinge shooting through her body. She hid her thoughts behind a quick murmur of thanks and a smile.

Outside the diner, the parking lot had been cleared of snow. The sky was clear, but it was bitterly cold. It was January, after all. Her breath fogged in the crisp air. Mary pulled on her gloves and flipped her coat collar up. In her haste to meet Laurie, she'd left her scarf at home.

"We can drive there together in my car," Brad said. "I'll bring you back when we're done."

"You have a rental?"

He pointed to a dark SUV. "C'mon. I'm an excellent driver."

She had to speed up her pace to catch up with him. He walked fast, his lanky legs crossing the cleared, snow-plowed parking lot quickly. He walked like a man who knew where he was going and knew what he wanted.

5

BRAD HAD FELT PROTECTIVE OF MARY EVER SINCE THE day she'd been running late for class and collided with him in the hallway of the high school. Her notebook, papers, and books had spilled out of her arms and landed on the shiny, waxed floor. He'd bent down to retrieve them, and saw a sketchpad opened to a drawing of a looming rock monument rising toward the sky, in a clearing surrounded by green space and trees. A flock of birds flew overhead, and circular clouds floated across a blue sky. They'd both reached for the pad, and in doing so, their hands had connected, their outstretched fingers touched, sending an electrical jolt.

He'd picked up the sketchpad and asked if it was hers, staring into her luminous brown eyes, opened wide. His heart slowed in mid-beat, and everything froze, blocking out the surrounding sounds, blurring movements around them, fading away everything except what he saw clearly—her beautiful face, a rush of redness on her cheeks, and her lips slightly parted. In that instant, he lost his heart and fell in love. He opened and closed his mouth without speaking.

She'd been flustered and had blushed, snatching her sketchpad, slamming it shut with a thump, and shoving it into her book bag.

Her face had been inches from his, and for what seemed like the longest time, their eyes stayed locked. Her warm breath caressed his cheek, as innocent as the first white layer of snow touching the ground.

He hadn't told her—or anyone. He didn't even understand why he felt that way, or what just happened. That day, they'd connected. But she started dating Jim, his friend, whom he'd never betray. Brad moved away and kept a watchful eye from afar, and on the occasional visits back to town, he was able to catch sight of her in person. He wasn't ready to give her up to Jim. But she wasn't his to give up.

Brad kept tabs on Jim and Mary through the grapevine. They'd been going together since the end of senior year. As far as he knew, Mary had dated little before Jim. She was shy, and a homebody. She didn't go bar-hopping. He, on the other hand, was a man about town. He was tall, dark, and handsome. He knew he exuded confidence, which in and of itself was sexy.

He'd skirted any attachments, real or pretend, until he met Kell, the woman he'd taken to Laurie's wedding as his fake plus one. She was a match for him—and his opposite. Icy blonde hair and frosty cold, while he was dark-haired and fiery warm. In the confidence area, she was ahead by a smidge. He admired her and almost feared her at the same time. It was a challenge, and he wanted her on his side.

He glanced at Mary. She'd been quiet on the drive, looking out the car window pensively.

"Hey, you cold?"

She shrugged and turned her head toward him, then looked away.

"I can turn up the heat," he said, his hand reaching for the dial.

"No, it's just right. Thank you," she said, softly.

He thought he heard a trace of nostalgia or sadness in her voice.

"I've forgotten how this place looks, the vast expanse of land," he said.

"You grew up here."

"And I left. I spend my days, and most nights, working behind four walls. In a city with cold concrete, high-rise buildings, and skyscrapers."

"What about the weekends? You can take off, get away from the city."

"I wish! I usually work on the weekends, too."

"You don't have any free time?" She frowned.

"What little free time I have…"

"You party and date?"

He snorted. "More like go to work events. Oblig-atory. I show up, make the rounds, then I leave."

"Are you forgetting something?" she teased.

"What do you mean?"

"I bet you meet beautiful women at the parties. Seems like you'd be having a lot of fun."

"I'm... well, sometimes I do happen to have a woman or two on each arm."

"You mean dates?"

"No—"

He rushed to reply, to deny relationships, but stopped. Those women turned out to be one-nighters. How could he explain that to her?

He coughed. "Not exactly. I guess you could call them dates. Short ones."

It didn't sound glamorous, the way he made it out to be. All work and no play made for a dull person.

Brad cleared his throat, changing the subject. "About the tiny houses... they'll be constructed in a new development solely for tiny homes. We've divided the land into multiple smaller lots, which made it less expensive, and we'll order building materials in bulk," he said, his voice bursting with renewed energy and passion.

"I can see the attraction," Mary said. "For those people who don't want to live in densely-packed buildings, tiny houses mean they'd still be able to afford homes on postage-sized pieces of land with grassy yards."

"Yes, and this will be a community for like-minded folks who want to live in tiny homes."

"Do you enjoy the outdoors?" Mary asked.

"Not in the city. We have some parks, but it gets crowded. Everyone wants the space and brings their dogs, too."

"Mind telling me where we're going now?"

"It's not far."

6

MARY HAD GROWN UP HERE WITH KATIE AND HAD SPENT all of her life in this small town. It was nestled in the foothills of the mountains and was as picturesque as a postcard. Indeed, it was on a postcard in the gift shop for tourists. The familiar landscape brought comfort and a good feeling. She was a local, always had been.

The tourists stopped here on the way to the big city. The town boasted two gas stations, one on each end of the town, on opposite sides of the coming and going traffic. It had one main street with stores crowded on both sides. A few buildings were on the off streets, but most everything one wanted was on the main thoroughfare.

She remembered the favorite places for kids to hang out—the drugstore fountain, the bakery, and the candy store where she had bought chocolates that were still her favorites. Most after-school activities were within walking distance. Somebody would know somebody who'd give them a ride home. The thing about being older was that they didn't worry about taking the yellow school bus, like the little kids. They had fun in those good ol' days. Would he remember?

She sneaked a glance at Brad. His thick head of hair was tousled and loose. His gorgeous profile—the sexy, masculine stubble, strong-shaped nose, and perfect, beautiful lips. Mmmm... kissable lips. When he smiled, the lines around his eyes crinkled.

She let her gaze linger, drawn to him. Brad had dressed casually today. He looked different—relaxed and approachable. When he was dressed in his expensive suits and immaculately groomed, there was a different aura, a glimmer of toughness and grit to take on calculated risks. Maybe it was her imagination. Maybe she'd be out of place in that world. Maybe it was the persona he had to project in the business world in order to survive. He'd succeeded. He had money, connections, and more. But those things weren't what interested her. She had looked deep into his brown eyes and met warmth and kindness.

Mary relaxed as he drove, sliding into a world where they talked easily, and he allowed her to slip briefly behind his tough exterior. She'd caught a glimpse today, and what she saw, she liked. No, she wanted.

Maybe it was the way his eyes lit up and his words rushed together when he talked about the project. His face became animated. It was spilling out of him, each word tossed out as fast as the next.

What was it he mentioned? Green space, tiny homes, and, oh, an organic garden. Each piece of it could be a project. Perhaps he needed to tailor it down a bit. Was his goal to build affordable housing and preserve open green space? How would it look with walking trails, a village park, and picnic tables? And a community gathering place? The options were varied and decisions would have to be made. Brad would make them.

Mary turned these thoughts in her head. Her heart thumped while thinking ahead to the project. *Silly girl*, she chided herself. He just wanted to discuss it and bounce off ideas. Period. He hadn't asked for their help, and Laurie did most of the talking early on, asking him questions and making comments. Brad had looked straight at Laurie, who sat opposite him. After she hastily excused herself, he'd directed his attention to Mary. She wasn't into small talk, especially with a man who had seemed more like a stranger to her. The years had flown by, and they were no longer in high school.

7

Brad was lost in thought as he drove. Why was Laurie so particular about the time when she called him? Most people would just say meet them on the hour or the half-hour. Not Laurie. She had been specific about the time. It was fifteen minutes after the hour. He had joked, "You mean on the hour?" Nope, she was serious. She made him repeat the time and emphasized she expected punctuality.

He'd set his watch alarm and walked into the diner precisely at a quarter after ten this morning, after arriving five minutes early and waiting in his car until his appointed time came. He'd been amused and played along. The words were on the tip of his tongue —half joking, half reproachful—about the hassle she was putting him through. But he almost bit his tongue when he realized Laurie wasn't alone. He'd held back, hesitating. Was she finishing up with another meeting?

He checked the clock on his watch. He'd been right on time.

It occurred to him now that maybe Laurie wasn't flaky. She was the opposite. Why would she go to all the trouble with the time? It didn't look like Mary was leaving as he arrived. She had a mouthful of food, and there was still plenty on her plate. He saw her eyebrows raised, almost as if she was just as surprised to see him.

If Mary was just as surprised, then they were both in the dark. He jerked his head to look at her now. It must have been all Laurie. Her idea, her plan. Brad had only a brief conversation with Laurie at the wedding when she asked how he was doing. His answer was short, including a sentence about the project. He didn't elaborate. It was then that Laurie said they could finish the conversation tomorrow and suggested they meet over breakfast at the diner. He didn't have any plans in the morning. It suited him just fine. He'd been polite and agreed. Besides, it'd been a while since he'd spent time with Laurie, and he was looking forward to doing a bit of catch-up, too. Previously, he had come back for her wedding, and she'd left for her honeymoon during the reception.

He was one of the few left in the old crowd who was still single. One by one, the others had gotten married. Now it was just him, Mary, and Jim who were left. Well, the other two had been expected to get married. And if they had, he'd have been the last holdout.

He wasn't in a hurry to get hitched. The business had kept him busy, and he traveled a lot. Besides, he'd known plenty of women, and truth be told, he hadn't met anyone he'd like to spend the rest of his life with. Sure, he liked them, some better than others. But none, except for Kell, had come close. And when he realized his mistakes and error in judgment with her, it further cemented his resolve.

Yet a part of him had been joyous when Mary and Jim had broken up. He didn't wish them ill, of course. But he secretly wished Mary wouldn't marry Jim, and if it had come to pass and they had gotten to the altar, he would have—well, he didn't want to go there.

He knew he wasn't ready to settle down, and what would have happened if he made any declaration to her? If he couldn't fulfill his promise, then he'd break her heart. He could not and would not do it. He couldn't bear to hurt her like that. The years had gone by, and he'd watched her from afar. Occasionally, he'd hear about her or her family. He'd known Katie, too. They'd all been friends at school and grown up together. He'd almost confided in Katie that he liked her sister, but he caught himself in time. It was so childish and long ago.

It was all wistful thinking on his part. Mary wasn't his. He'd never made his true feelings known. All these years, she hadn't found out how he felt about her. He'd told no one, least of all Mary. She'd been blissfully unaware, attending to her own life, going on as if he wasn't in it. As if he wasn't in the picture. And he wasn't. For Brad hadn't had the courage to tell her. And he wasn't ready to tell her now.

There had been a few times when he almost gave it away. He'd worked up enough nerve—well, almost—to tell her he liked her. Not a full declaration, but what he could live with. Baby steps, nothing to wow her or bowl her over or frighten her away. Just a brief whisper in her ear. Then he'd run away. Oh, but it would've been the cowardly thing to do. Brad wasn't like that. He believed in honesty, and when a man said something, it should mean something, and it should be binding. Words shouldn't be said on a whim or as a fleeting thought. Words had meaning, and when delivered, he'd stand by them. He'd live by his words. Those words he never uttered to Mary and kept in his heart.

8

Mary's heart skipped a beat when they arrived at Craig's Rock, her favorite place. It was an outcropping of rocks, and at the top of the mountain was a massive table rock. She remembered the first time she'd seen it; how awestruck she'd been. She was a child then, thinking the rocks were created by God on this sacred piece of land. It had become a landmark, with trails up the mountain.

Off to the side, someone had erected a plaque. As a child, she'd come with her family. They'd brought a picnic and stayed all day. It didn't seem scary then, and the children had played hide-and-go-seek among the rocks, running in between and around them. Yells and shrieks of laughter filled the air as the kids romped on the rocky terrain. It was a happy place, a special place. She'd carved Brad's initials on a spot on the rock, next to her initials.

She sighed as memories faded to the present.

Outside, the tree branches stood stiff, with ice coating them like frosting. She shivered.

Brad leaned in, eyebrows drawing together. "You cold? I can turn up the heat."

"No." She gave a slight smile. "I just… I haven't been here for a while."

"We don't have to get out and walk. Your feet will freeze in those shoes."

Mary had put on her regular shoes for breakfast at the diner and left her warm boots at home in the shoe rack by the front door.

"I'll be fine." She pulled the passenger door latch, stepped out of the car, and walked. Her fingers and toes rebelled at the cold temperature. She was grateful the snow had covered the rocks, leaving a thin shimmer of white glaze over the scene. Her carved initials would be safely hidden under the blanket of snow and ice. In a few months, spring would change the landscape and bring out the beauty of it all. By then, the earth would soften.

This place was her favorite to visit, a wondrous place for a child. It brought back memories of her childhood and later in her teens—before Katie left and moved to the city, before her dad fell sick and died, before their momma became heartsick, and later when she couldn't walk well. It was different now; nothing could bring back those days. She hadn't returned for so long. But time had a way of healing, and maybe it was time again, after all those years. Maybe Brad had the right idea, and this was the time, now. She sighed, sniffing back tears.

Mary's memories slipped back to another time, when Brad's face had been inches away, and she had felt the warmth of his breath.

"Um, excuse me," he had mumbled, leaning closer as he picked up her sketchpad.

She had a good look at his face, the smoothness of his cheek, and a nick or two where the teenager needed more practice shaving. Thick, long lashes fanned his eyes. She'd smiled and forgiven him on the spot for bumping into her. They had touched accidently, and she felt a tingling. When his hand moved, she'd reached out and held it for a moment, as a friend would do to comfort someone or ease their tension. "Thank you," she'd said.

He was Jim's friend and her friend too—and her secret crush in grade school. He was the shy one. Brad didn't speak to her much. She couldn't remember how many times he did talk to her directly. There had been only a few occasions when they were together with a group that he'd chimed in with a remark or two. He wasn't loose with his lips and didn't rattle on about things of no consequence. He was a thoughtful person and kept things to himself. She liked that.

Brad didn't criticize or belittle or make fun of others. Like the time someone walked into a glass wall and smacked their face. Everyone had laughed, even Mary. It was involuntary, almost, but she had glanced around, embarrassed, and noticed Brad was quiet. He didn't make fun of him. Instead, he'd walked up to the guy to check on how he was doing. He put his arm around the guy's back and whispered some words. She remembered this, that he had reacted differently than the other kids. Caring, calm, collected.

"Earth to Mary," Brad said, his frosted breath cascading in the air as she stood before the rock formation.

She shook her head, clearing away her thoughts.

"You okay?" he asked.

Mary nodded, walking on, clearing snow from a flat surface. She sat, and gestured to the space beside her. "Let's sit here for a while."

The view was magnificent. They were at the top of the hill, the rock formations jutting out like an old, stooped man. Garbled and twisted tree roots and plants sought out the crevices and found footholds. Before them, the beautiful landscape stretched as far as she could see. It was a cold, crisp day. No clouds were in sight. Isolated, sitting on the flat table of the rock ridge, the whole world was before them. It was spectacular.

She sighed, letting go a long exhale. The warm air escaped into the wild, into the icy beauty of the land.

"You know, I've never come in the winter," Brad said.

"Me neither. The starkness and the whiteness... it's so—"

"Breathtaking, right?"

She nodded.

They sat together, a comfortable silence between them. The wind whistled, and the tree branches shook gently. Somewhere, a bird cawed, or it sounded like it. The sun was out, casting away the shadows and spreading its brightness over the land. It wasn't enough to warm the ice or melt the snow. Yet a warmth spread through Mary, even though her feet were cold and wetness seeped through her soggy socks. She didn't care. She couldn't believe she was here, sitting beside Brad, in this most heavenly piece of land, the most beautiful of God's creations. God's country, they'd say. She smiled.

9

Old feelings surfaced for Brad. Mixed feelings he'd repressed since senior year. His stomach knotted as the familiar pang of hurt reared its ugly head, and anger and a sense of betrayal gripped his core over what Mary did to him. It woke up a sleeping dragon he'd put to slumber years ago. Only thing was, the dragon was fully awake now, and his fiery breath pumped up. His bottled-up feelings came to the surface, rising from the depths of his mind to a fully awakened beast as old wounds reopened amidst pulsing, red-hot desires.

He was aware of the pang in his heart at the diner when he caught a whiff of Mary's sweet scent as he leaned in closer to put her coat on. He'd noticed the swell of her chest thrusting out from under her knit sweater before glancing away quickly. He felt a sensation as their knees touched when he shifted in the chair, parting his legs and bumping into hers. He'd smiled weakly when she called out his name, her lips parting. He'd trembled from her touch as her fingertips brushed his hand.

He yearned for more. He yearned to hear her speak his name, call out for him, want him. He yearned for her kiss, her longing. He yearned to satisfy her and yet leave her wanting for more. He yearned to connect with her as he'd never connected with another human being before.

Not a rushed, quick fling. Not the emptiness afterward. Not the euphoric high that never satisfied completely.

He'd lived with the ache in his heart for years, never letting on to others. It would've been wrong to change her world then, to convince her of his love, to break her away from Jim. He couldn't have lived with himself afterward. Forcing himself that way wasn't in his nature.

At night, she was in his dreams. In them, he relived the way she gazed into his eyes that day in high school, her large eyes wide open toward him. He felt in that moment there wasn't anyone else in the world besides the two of them. Her gaze said volumes. It cried out to him; he rejoiced in it. A look of teen angst, wonder, and the adoration of a crush. It was wondrous. His heartbeat had quickened, and he felt a tingling. He was transfixed. His feet stuck to the floor like lead, the force of it taking him by surprise. It was unexplainable, exhilarating, and brought on a bravery he'd never felt before. It emboldened him and made him want to rise up to the world, fearless and unstoppable. It felt great.

Then, the dream would be gone, almost as quickly as it came.

He had wanted her. All of her—body, mind, and soul. He wanted to be with her every day. To wake up beside her. For her to be the last person he saw when his head hit the pillow. To eat, to sleep, to be with her. That was, until she broke his heart.

10

———

On the drive back to town, thoughts swirled in Mary's head. Why did Brad choose the rock formation? Was it because he wanted her to see it in winter? Did he remember that day, in the hallway of the high school, when they collided? When her sketchpad fell to the floor, spilling to the page she'd drawn of the rocks?

She blushed, turning her cheeks away to glance out the passenger window. It was presumptuous of her to think he'd remember something that took place in the span of a few seconds more than ten years ago. She shook her head at the thought.

The day was bright and crisp, the sunlight bouncing across the snow-covered landscape. Up ahead, a sign pointed to Winter Village, a spot for tourists.

"There," she said, pointing to the cute sign. "Turn right. I want to show you this place."

Brad's eyes followed her finger and spotted the curve in the road and the turn-off. "What is this?"

"Oh, you'll see," she squealed, straining her seat belt in excitement. "Follow the sign. The road will wind around a group of buildings." As they got closer, a cluster of log cabins came into view. Snow-covered, they stood out from the woods, like pioneer cabins. The old west and small-town look. It wasn't a replica of a whole town, only three buildings still decorated with festive holiday cheer, with wreaths, bells, and lighted outdoor displays.

"Isn't this cute?" Mary blurted out, one hand releasing her seat belt, and the other on the door handle as Brad pulled into the parking lot and found a good spot not too far from the cabins. She stepped out of the car. "I'll show you around."

He nodded, surveying the scene as they walked. "This must be new?"

"Yes, it was built in the last three years. You haven't been?"

"No. First time I've seen this. This town has changed since high school."

"But you've been back."

"Quick trips, holidays, weddings, those events. Obligatory, you know."

She threw him a quick smile. "You didn't really have to, unless you wanted to, too."

"That's right. Nobody forced me. Now, if you're talking about the high school reunion, I missed that on purpose."

"I'd glad you came back for Katie's wedding," she said.

"Hey, it was New Year's Day—what better way to celebrate?" He attempted a toast with an imaginary glass.

"Happy New Year, Brad," she giggled, rolling her eyes. "Did you do any work after the wedding?"

"Hmph. I was tempted. It's a holiday weekend. Even I knew it. I gave myself the night off and ordered room service."

"Oh, you didn't invite me." She pouted, lips pursed.

He studied her face, as if staring at it would provide answers.

She enjoyed this, and she was surprised at how easy it was to flirt with Brad. He was down to earth, like before he left ten years ago. Ten and a half, to be more exact. Who would have guessed he'd be more handsome than he was in high school? Smooth, assured, and irresistible. She wanted to rake her nails over his rough shadow of a beard and run them through his thick head of hair, then glide them down the tip of his nose and slide her finger on his luscious lips. Mary daydreamed, letting the delicious thoughts run wild.

"I like your smile," he said.

She blushed. He caught her thinking and smiling about him. Oh man, he better not be able to read minds.

"And here I thought it was my charming personality."

"Don't forget your graceful neck and beautiful hands," he said teasingly.

"It's hard to pick, isn't it? How about my feet?" She lifted her coat and playfully stuck her foot out, wiggling her shoe and throwing out her hands.

Mary did such a good job at it, putting all her gusto into the to-and-fro action of her foot, that she lost her balance. She shrieked, arms waving, and swayed. Her body hung in balance for a second. Then she toppled, giving one last grasp into thin air as she fell backward. She let out a scream and closed her eyes, expecting the hard plop when the weight of her body hit the ground. But it didn't happen.

Brad swung into action and whipped his arms under her. He faltered under her weight and bulkiness, enhanced by the heavy coat she wore. But he managed to hold her up and break her fall.

"I got you now," he said, his labored breaths escaping into the cold air as his arms provided a pair of strong supports under her.

Mary opened her eyelids and peeked out from her lashes, her eyes lighting on Brad's scrunched face. She rubbed the side of her face where his scrubby beard had scraped her cheek, then allowed him to pull her up. When she stood, she was still trembling. She wrapped her arms around his neck and squeezed, giving him a grateful hug.

"Thank you," she stuttered, not letting go. Not just yet.

"Lucky catch," Brad said, grinning ear to ear.

"I'm the lucky one."

She meant it.

11

———————

Brad had a view of Mary close up and caught a faint whiff of her scent, a light fragrance. He didn't want to release her. Wanted to keep his arms wrapped around her.

He had a fall in high school. He had stayed late one day, and it was the dead of winter. The dusk fell early. He'd lost track of time and ran out of the building to the parking lot where he'd parked his car. They'd cleared the sidewalk, but the lot was a sheet of ice. He'd slipped, and his feet flew out from under him. There was nothing he could do. He could still hear it now, the crack of his skull as it hit the icy surface. The throbbing pain. He'd sat there, holding his head. Not getting up. It happened in a few seconds, but at the time, it seemed to stretch into minutes while he stayed still, bent over the ice. He'd gotten up, his legs wobbly at first, and shuffled toward his car, taking slow, careful steps. He was able to go home that day. When he woke up the next morning, he thanked God.

Ever since then, he'd been more careful of the ice and snow. He'd learned his lesson, not just walking but also driving. He took driver's ed at school, one of the few remaining years before they stopped doing it.

Brad gazed down at Mary. She looked so lovely. At this moment, she was safe in his arms instead of on the slick, snow-covered icy ground. His heart ached with the desire to keep her safe and to protect her with all his might.

Mary hadn't protested when she realized he was holding her. Her body had tightened, then gone limp. He felt her tremble through her clothes and coat. She let him hold her and hugged him.

Brad loosened up a bit, enough to check her out.

"Are you okay?" he said, not realizing his voice sounded hoarse until he spoke.

She gazed into his eyes unwaveringly.

He tightened his grip involuntarily, bringing her closer.

She put her arms around his neck again, laid her head on his shoulder, and leaned into him.

Brad felt his racing heartbeat and an outpouring of tenderness for her.

They'd been friends ever since grade school, for more than two decades. Nothing more had ever been said about his feelings.

His original plans had been to leave town after the wedding, rushing back. But it was the holiday weekend still, and the employees were off on leave. Brad should be, too. Part of him thought it was the perfect chance to work, uninterrupted, with the entire floor of the office all to himself. It was tempting.

But his heart quickened at this new temptation—one he hadn't planned on, hadn't expected, and couldn't resist. Her gorgeous, large eyes and the way her lashes fluttered from panic... he'd been the one to calm her, to quiet the anxiety and fear in her eyes. He'd been at the right place at the right time. He'd saved her from falling into the snow and a possible concussion if her head had hit the ground. Was it frozen earth under the snow and ice or hard concrete or gravel with sharp edges? She could have been injured.

He sucked in his breath. He was here now. Resisting the temptation before his eyes. Biting his lips to keep from crushing hers. What had gotten into him? *Take ahold of yourself*, he admonished. *Stop acting like a silly teenager. Don't make a fool of yourself. And Brad, wipe that silly grin off your face.*

He lowered his head, and in his mind, he pressed his lips gently, meeting her soft, cold-chilled lips, warming them, and she pressed back, responding to his kiss. Gentle, smooth, and slow.

A droplet of fluid dripped on his cheek. What was it? He felt the drop run down his face and teeter precipitously on his chin. He wiped it away. The teardrop, he realized, was his.

He turned his attention to the present and walked

with her, taking small steps and guarding her. "There are icy patches. Be careful."

She shot him a grateful glance.

They made their way to the brightly lit village. It consisted of two larger structures and a much smaller hut with barely enough room enough for the vendor to set up a kettle of warm apple cider. Next to it was a commercial hot-water dispenser and packets of hot chocolate.

Brad eased to the counter and turned to Mary. "Would you like a cup of warm cider?"

She nodded enthusiastically. "Yes, I'd like one. I'll find us a place to sit."

"Make that two, please," he said to the vender, ordering the drinks and dropping a five-dollar bill on the counter. "Keep the change."

"I'll put it in the tip jar," the vendor said. "It goes to my dog for doggie treats."

Brad saw him wink before he made the change. It was all for a good cause. He brought the drinks over to Mary. Scattered in the village center were a few long tables. These were the community-style tables where people could sit together and eat and drink and talk.

Brad sat next to Mary, instead of across the table, and handed her the drink.

"Thank you." She nodded, bringing her face to the rising wisp of steam over the cup. Mary sipped tentatively, testing the temperature of the drink.

"It's good?"

"So good. Yours?"

Brad quickly took a gulp of his drink and swallowed, almost burning his mouth, and flinched.

He laughed it off. Didn't want to show any weakness to her. "It's good. I haven't had apple cider for a while. It's yummy."

"Yeah, this is what I love this time of the year. I'm glad you got it for me."

"I'm glad you like it," he said, noting her comment and adding to his mental list of what she liked. It was easy talking to her, and he moved closer, hoping she wouldn't notice. It felt good, sitting here with her, having another quiet moment to talk, and to laugh a bit. She was every bit as lovely as he'd imagined, and he was glad she was enjoying herself.

12

THE TABLE WHERE MARY SAT OFFERED A PERFECT VIEW
of the festive village, where more people had gathered
in the afternoon. In the background, music blared over
speakers. The sky was a crisp blue, not a cloud above.
The layer of snow on top reflected the sunlight.

Mary sipped her apple cider, her gloved hands
clasped around the cup. A soft gurgling sound escaped
from her belly.

"You hungry?" Brad asked. "I think they have
popcorn and candy bars at the drink stand."

She smiled, giving him a playful tap and hiding her
embarrassment. "No, I'm fine. But I think you need to
get your ears checked."

"My hearing is perfectly fine. I know what you're
trying to do."

"My belly's fine, too. I'm enjoying the view and the
people."

"It's nice, isn't it?" He sighed, scanning the

picturesque scene. "They sure didn't have this when we were growing up."

Mary nodded.

The music paused, and an announcement came over the speakers that some skates were still available for rent. People moved to the other end of the buildings, toward the ice-skating rink. Off to the side was a rental counter with a selection of skates.

Mary jumped up and tugged Brad's arm. "C'mon, let's go have a look."

She led the way, following the sounds of pop music and laughter. Already, the rink was filling up. Someone shouted when one of the kids stumbled. It didn't take long to figure out who was new at it, and who was more seasoned. It didn't matter. They were all having fun, even when they ended up with their butts on the ice rink.

"I dare you," Brad said.

"Wait, you know how to skate?"

"You want to see? I'm game. Are you?"

Mary hesitated. She wasn't actually very good, but Brad probably wouldn't know that. Was he daring her to skate or wanting her to join the fun? The rink was filling up with ice skaters as the upbeat music boomed.

"I don't think you want to find out." She was testing him and daring him to do it, too.

"I bet I can out-skate you," he said.

"Try me," she said, pulling up the legs of her pants. "Let's check and see if they have rentals in our sizes."

At the counter, Mary inquired about skates. Fortunately, their sizes were in stock. Brad paid for the rentals, and they got on the rink, warming up first, then blending in with the flow of skaters. Someone had turned up the music, and it was blasting. She held up her gloves to her ears and made a funny face.

Brad laughed and skated right past her, much to the astonishment of Mary, who just lost her bet.

13

———

IT HADN'T OCCURRED TO BRAD THAT SKATING COULD BE so much fun. Not that he hadn't skated before. Mary was a good sport. He could tell she tried hard, and each time she fell on her butt, she got up again. He kept an eye on her and was ready to give a hand when needed. But Mary was not a quitter. She pulled on her big-girl pants and started up again, time after time. It was refreshing to see how determined she was, and how she never stayed down for too long.

It was a good workout. Brad wanted to stay in the rink as long as Mary didn't give up. He'd slowed down and started to skate with her, building a rhythm and speed to match hers. Eventually, they skated together and made it once around the rink without interruption.

Brad loosened up and relaxed. He had been away for so long, he missed the small-town activities and the things he'd liked to do as a kid. There were many opportunities all year long, with summer being the busiest. Growing up, he took the seasons for granted. He realized now he couldn't live year-round on the beach. If someone asked whether he was a beach or mountain guy, it'd be mountains for sure. Not to say he didn't like the sand and sea—who didn't? But his heart was in these mountains. He would never stray too far.

He'd traded the simpler, quieter life for the excitement and thrills of the city and what it had to offer to a young man making his way up in the business world. That world seemed far away and out of sight now, as the serenity of the hills and their beauty struck him. The feeling was indescribable.

He had turned his cell phone ringer off. Beauty like this should be undisturbed. He wasn't just thinking about the landscape, but also Mary. If anyone had asked him a day ago what he'd be doing, he'd have spouted off the usual answer mindlessly while multitasking, hunched over his laptop.

The phone vibrated again, although he had put it on silent. Irritated, he resisted the urge to pull it out and see who was calling. He should have left it in the car, and he would, the next time he got a chance. Nothing was going to spoil this beautiful day.

He looked up at the sky, blue and clear, the sun a welcome sight. He perked up, catching up to Mary and rejoining her on the rink.

14

Mary was wondering where Brad was. She had gone around the rink twice by herself and didn't want him to watch over her. It was a relief he'd left her alone. It also signaled, at least to Mary, that he was secure enough in her ability to skate and her progress after his mini-lessons.

She kept an eye out for him to rejoin her. It was about two circles around the rink later when he caught up alongside her.

"Hey, everything okay?" Mary blushed, too late to choke the words back and not wanting him to think she had missed him.

"Yeah."

"Not trying to sneak in a quick business meeting, huh?"

"Nope, not even a call." Brad patted his cell halfway sticking out of his jacket and pushed it down lower. He changed the subject quickly, turning toward her and watching her skating technique. "You're doing better than I thought."

"Oh, you want me to thank you for those mini-lessons?"

"Heck no. I'm just proud of you." He grinned.

Mary watched his Adam's apple move up and down, and slid her eyes down to his solid chest, broad shoulders, and tapering waist. His leather belt and metal clasp held up blue jeans that looked new. Even his casual clothes appeared to have come from a shopping bag recently. Did a man like him really have time for shopping, or was everything ordered online and could be had with a click of a button? Surely, this man didn't go to the mall and hadn't set foot in any fancy boutique stores. But he had good taste in clothes. She wondered if it extended to women.

Mary had kept her secret crush on Brad to herself and didn't confide in anyone—least of all her sister. Maybe it was because it felt warm and thrilling and super special to hold it close. Maybe she didn't want to feel the sting of her sister's retort or anger, for Katie could be sharp and hurtful with her remarks. Maybe she didn't want to turn on Katie's competitive edge, something she sensed could happen. Mary was shy, especially with matters of the heart. She tucked it away and didn't do anything with it.

As the years went by, they continued to be friends, and the crush dissipated, pushed to the recesses of her mind. She hadn't acted on it and eventually put it out of her mind. Then, in high school, she'd had fewer interactions with Brad. They didn't have as many classes together, and after-school activities kept them busy. Occasionally they hung out, always in a group, getting together after school whenever they had an afternoon free. Their free time got rarer after they both started working part-time jobs.

Mary forgot about her childish thoughts as she grew out of those phases, both physically and mentally. Adolescence was an awkward and confusing time for her. When she hung out with friends in her free time, sometimes Brad would show up, but more often, he'd be busy or working. Mary concentrated on her studies, but often found herself thinking about him as raging hormones, mood changes, and irritability toyed with her emotions. It was only in her senior year that she did some dating, mostly within her circle of friends and casual acquaintances. And on that fateful day when she made a decision, right before senior prom, her hormones were out of whack.

After graduation, Brad moved away. She'd known he'd leave town. It was no surprise. He'd talked about college and big plans afterward.

It was a bittersweet time. After that summer, things would never be the same. Tearful goodbyes, hugs, and every excuse for parties until the end, with sweet promises. And then they were gone. There were others who had stayed in town—those who couldn't get away or didn't want to leave, like Mary.

Mary carved out her life in the same place where she was born and raised. In the same house she grew up in. She would not make it out of town then, and she gave herself permission to be kind to herself. The fire didn't burn in her belly to leave. It wasn't the only route in her life, and the timing wasn't right for her.

Mary had been the good daughter. The dependable one. She'd stayed in town and lived with her parents for a brief period after high school. She got a job as a waitress, saved some money, and soon after, she moved to a small apartment close by. She went to community college, taking one course per semester while she worked. It was affordable, and she could handle the pace with her schedule. She studied hard, made good grades, and graduated with honors.

Her parents were so proud of her. It was before Dad got sick and died. When they were still a family together. It was before Momma was heartbroken by grief, a pale ghost of her former self. Mary was at Dad's bedside when he passed and comforted her momma afterward. Yet the depth of Momma's grief was unfathomable to a daughter who was fresh to pain herself. Together, they somehow made it through the first hours, days, and then weeks after he died. Mary never complained or said it was unfair to take on this load. Katie had been Dad's favorite, yet she wasn't by his side when he passed.

Where had the last ten years gone? Now, at almost thirty years of age, Mary shook off the sadness and a tinge of bitterness at Father Time.

Without bidding, tears wet her cheeks. A bittersweet, feeling-sorry-for-herself moment. Mary swiped her glove across her face, rubbing away traces of wetness. She needed a moment to herself.

"Hey, I'm done for the day. Heading over there," she said to Brad as she skated away, pointing across the rink toward the ladies' restroom, drawing attention away from her moist cheeks. A metal sign hung over the door of the small building, which was made of the same hewn logs as the other structures.

"Okay, I'm going for a couple more rounds, then I'll meet you back at the table where we were," Brad said.

Mary skated to the bench at the exit and sat, removing her skates and returning them to the kid at the rental counter. She made her way to the ladies' restroom, stepping with care, relieved there was no line. She was quick and washed her hands and dried them with a towel before she walked out.

She pushed the door open, half expecting to see Brad. But the guy looming in the doorway was scruffy, like he hadn't shaven, and wearing a wrinkled shirt with a lopsided collar sticking out from under his coat.

"Huh?" she gasped, sounding weird to herself as she recognized the man. Her ex-boyfriend, Jim. "What are you doing here?"

"I oughta ask you... what... are you." His speech was slurred.

She smelled the odor of his alcohol breath in the chilly air. He'd probably vomited in the men's room, she thought, as her eyes spotted a few remnants clinging to the front of his shirt. It was so unlike Jim, who presented himself in public as a quiet, reserved man. Tall, good-looking, and not one to make a ruckus or get into a drunken brawl.

"I think you've had too much to drink." She spoke calmly, in a quiet whisper. This wasn't the same man she knew. The Jim she knew controlled everything and everyone—especially her. His expectations were clear, and she learned over the years what they were. As long as she made peace and went along, everything was fine. He wanted a traditional girlfriend, and it was the same in a wife—obedient, stay-at-home, taking care of number one: Jim. It took her a long time to see it and to get it. He didn't hurt her or beat her. What he did left no physical scars.

What he offered was a comfortable life, and he wanted a woman he could command. If she didn't do his bidding, she knew the consequences.

She finally had the courage to break it off before Katie's wedding. She had made it clear to Jim, and he hadn't fought it when she told him. He had a sad, resigned look then. She had avoided him as much as possible, didn't return his calls, and didn't answer her door the one time he came by. Maybe it was seeing her at Katie's wedding yesterday that drove him to drink and unhinged him?

"No, not a..." He swayed and looked down at his bent knees. "What you gonna..."

"Here," Mary said, ducking under his arm and lifting it over her head, feeling the weight of his limp body. "Okay, lift your feet and walk with me. I can't carry you." She reshuffled his arm to position it closer and supported him as they walked toward the tables.

Jim wasn't a heavy man, yet it seemed like he was to Mary. He was slim, and of average weight and build. He worked at a garage repair shop, which was passed down by his father when he retired. Jim told her that ever since he could remember, he had watched his father fix almost anything. Although the garage was packed full of cars, folks brought other things to be fixed, like lawnmowers and bikes. He didn't know how it started or who brought the first item, but from the first satisfied customer, word spread, even though the sign had never changed—it still said "Dad's Garage." When his father retired, Jim kept the name out of respect for him, and the folks who had been customers for the past four decades. Luckily, Jim had inherited the genes, and he had a talent for the work. Work wasn't the only thing he'd inherited, though. Stubbornness and a stickler for old-fashioned traditions were instilled in the boy, too.

Mary flicked her head back; his head had wobbled, and curly hairs tickled her cheek. She struggled as he leaned hard on her. Was he aware, despite his seeming incoherence? She wasn't raised around folks who drank a lot and wasn't used to this type of behavior from anyone she knew—least of all Jim. A thought flashed, accompanied by a dash of guilt. Was it because she broke up with him?

15

AFTER ONE LAST SWISH AND GRINDING HIS SKATES TO A stop, Brad sat and took them off, returning the skates to the kid at the rental counter. He left a tip, sliding it under his skates. Taking a moment to stretch his legs on the ground, Brad surveyed the area, searching for Mary. She wasn't waiting for him at the tables, nor was she outside the women's facilities. Maybe she was waiting by the car? He picked up his feet and headed toward the parking lot.

A grunt caught his attention. Looking toward the source of the sound, his eyes tracked to his right to a bent figure—a limping woman straining under the weight of a man, making her way toward the tables. He blinked. The coat was familiar. Could it be... a chill ran down his spine. As he realized it was Mary, Brad rushed after her. It wasn't hard to catch up with her and the man she was lugging along. Upon closer inspection, it was none other than Jim.

Brad inhaled sharply. He instinctively pressed his palm on her shoulder to stop her and reached out with his other hand. "Here, let me help you." He pried Jim's arm from its tight wrap around her and transferred it to his shoulder.

"I think we should take him home. He's in no shape to drive," Mary said.

"But you were going the other way."

"I was going to sit down and wait for you. I don't have the keys." Taking a breath, she huffed and expelled the air.

"Do you know where he's parked?"

"His truck..."

"You show me."

"Maybe we should try to sober him up."

"He's too far gone. Let's get him home, and he can sleep it off." Brad shifted his weight and turned sideways, his pants pocket facing Mary. "Grab my keys, will you? You can unlock my car, and we'll leave his truck here."

"You sure you don't want to drive his truck? I'll lead the way there with your car."

Brad eyed her, chewing his lip thoughtfully. "It could work. You find his keys."

She searched Jim's pocket, patting it and hearing the clanging noise of keys jiggling against metal.

MARY PASSED Jim's keys to Brad.

He grunted, catching them with one hand, his lips pressed tight with concentration.

Together, they managed to get Jim settled and buckled into the passenger seat of his truck.

She drove Brad's car, leading the way to Jim's place a short distance away. He lived a few doors down from the garage, a few easy strides to work every morning. When they arrived, Mary was relieved Jim was still out. She didn't want a scene, and certainly not in front of Brad.

They took Jim inside his home and carried him to the bedroom. They hoisted him onto his bed, took off his shoes, covered him with a blanket, and made him comfortable. Standing over him, Mary watched him sleep for a moment, then gestured to Brad, moving toward the door. Before she left the room, she turned off the light, then closed the door softly behind her.

"He'll need to sleep it off," Brad said.

She fidgeted with her hair, feeling awkward. Saying nothing. She slumped and backed up against the hallway wall.

"I'm sure he'll be fine," he said.

She nodded as her fingers clutched her sweater then smoothed it.

"Tell me what you're thinking," he said, his deep voice soothing and low.

Mary raised her eyes, watching his lips move. The words coming out were soft, warm, and rich, like well-seasoned wine. They poured out of his throat like velvet salve over a wound. She felt calm and trusting.

Her muscles relaxed. She sighed and let her breath out slowly.

"You know, when something is over, it isn't all cut and dry." She kept her voice low so as not to wake up Jim, although chances of it were miniscule.

Brad appeared to have read her mind. He shook his head. "I don't want to ask or pry. Jim's my friend, too."

Her eyes flicked toward the bedroom door, checking it, looking to make sure it was still closed.

Brad noticed her glance. "Are you worried about him?"

"He's, uh, it's not like him. You know, he likes to be in control."

"He's had too much to drink. Let him sleep it off."

"He's not a habitual drinker."

"I get why you're here..."

"Yeah, we were all friends, even before I dated Jim."

"Those were the good ol' days back in school."

"What happened to us, after we went our separate ways?" Her eyes softened. "Did you ever wonder about the kids who stayed behind?"

Brad frowned. "I was in a hurry to get out, to go into the world. At the same time, I was afraid, but I didn't let it get to me." He paused.

"Did you ever wonder who were the lucky ones—the ones who got out or the ones who stayed?"

She gave a slight smile. It was quiet, so quiet she could hear Brad's exhale. They were so close, she felt his warm breath on her neck. Mary stared into his eyes, and they connected. Maybe a hundred seconds ticked by. She lost track of the time. It didn't matter.

BRAD RAISED his eyes and locked gazes with Mary. A strong current passed between them. Intense. Direct. Penetrating.

He dropped his eyelids and glanced down her face, traveling past her pert nose to her lips, parted just a sliver. Was it an invitation? Was she tantalizing him? Bewitching him with her allure? He bent his neck, stretching closer to her. His nose rubbed her cheek. Did she tremble and sigh?

"May I kiss you?" Brad whispered. He was an old-fashioned man at heart. Mary wasn't like the other girls, who were so available and ready. He wanted to treat her like a lady. She was special to him. He felt shy, rooted to his feet like a schoolboy. A flush crept on his cheeks, and a jolt shot through his body. His heart was thumping against his chest so loud that, surely, she could hear.

He tilted his head, waiting.

Her eyes glowed in the dim light of the hallway. There was no doubt what her answer was.

He wanted to kiss her, explore her lips, push them open wider until they clung to him. Pressing into them with a fierce fire that released into flames. Crazy thoughts dashed through his brain. Thoughts he'd suppressed. Wanton thoughts that had never seen the light of day. He wanted her now, right then and there.

His mind protested—it was crazy, in Jim's house, a few feet from where he was snoring. What if he woke up? The other part of his mind chastised him, saying not to worry about Jim, not even think about him. He was asleep, spread out on the bed. Jim was out of the picture now. Mary was going to be his. She was willing, and she had not protested. He could be gentle, take it slow. There was no need to hurry, soothed another voice. He could take all the time in the world. He had waited so long.

He bent his head down, tilting his chin for the right angle—and missed her lips.

She'd turned her head away. His lips grazed her cheek.

"Not here," she whispered, gently yet firm. "Not now."

16

THE SKY HAD TURNED GRAY AND CLOUDY WHEN MARY left Jim's house with Brad. Over the years, she'd been there countless times. Jim had preferred she come to his place rather than going to Mary's small apartment. It was really a matter of convenience, since it was so close to the garage. To get to Mary's place, he'd have to drive a couple of miles. It wasn't so far, but it meant he'd have to drive back home and then get up early at five thirty a.m. to get ready for work.

Mary hadn't minded in the early years. It became a habit to have dinner at his place during the week and spend time afterward watching a movie, or football game if it was a Monday or Thursday night.

Since Jim didn't cook, and he detested shopping, Mary would make a stop at the grocery store and pick up items for dinner before arriving. She'd prepare and cook what she bought, and set the table for two. Every once in a while, Jim would offer to help, and well, his help wasn't really helpful at all. In the end, the solution was for Jim to stay away from the kitchen when she was preparing meals. Mary liked to cook, and for a while, cooking for two was more fun than cooking for one.

Once in a while, Jim would wash the dishes. He didn't like to use the dishwasher because it was noisy. He didn't mind washing by hand, and scrubbing and rinsing. Sometimes it turned out to be a two-person task, with one washing and the other rinsing. By the time it was done, Mary was often tired and ready to go home.

At one point in their relationship, Jim had suggested, or rather asked point blank, why she didn't move in with him. Mary had thought about it more than once. She'd envisioned what life would be like living with him. But the more she mulled it over, the more it didn't sit well with her, the thought of losing the little bit of freedom, of independence, she had. Despite his urgings, the more he pressured her, the more she'd resisted.

"A nickel for your thoughts," Brad said, keys in hand as they approached his car.

Mary refocused and raised her eyes to his face.

"I'm afraid it won't be entertaining."

"You look a bit lost. How are you?"

She sighed heavily.

"Hey, I've got an idea," he said, his eyes sparkling.

She started to smile, knowing he was trying to cheer her up.

"Look, why don't we head out of town?"

"You mean, go now?" Mary said quietly.

"I know just the place we could go."

"Where?" She could barely keep the curiosity out of her voice. Maybe he should keep it a surprise and not tell her. On the other hand, she was dying to know. She preferred to know where she was going, and well, out of town sounded intriguing. Like it would be a fun, on-the-spot, adventurous thing to do. She didn't have any plans, and she had the time. It was still the holiday weekend, and she wanted to enjoy it.

"They've opened a new market square, a mixture of old and new buildings in an open-air village concept in the next town. Have you been there?"

"No, but I've been meaning to go check it out."

"Really?"

"I'd like to go."

"I think the place will still be decked out for the holidays, and it's open today. We can go see the lights and have fun."

"Perfect way to start the new year."

Mary picked up on his excitement, and her heart beat faster. She'd seen the advertisement in the paper, and the thought had crossed her mind to go. But what fun would it be to go by herself? Newly single instead of a longtime duo, Mary had been accustomed to having Jim around, even though he didn't like to go shopping or do spontaneous, adventurous things. He was a "stay home on the couch in front of the TV" person, and they rarely went out. They had in the beginning, but that was years ago. Jim didn't try toward the end, not for her. Not for himself either.

She refused to get stuck in a rut. Darn it, she still had life in her, and plenty of it. She still craved adventure, to see new places, and to have fresh experiences. She wasn't ready to give it all up before she was thirty —well, she was almost thirty, but not yet.

17

Brad didn't think before he opened his mouth. It happened as if his voice had a mind of its own. It amazed him when the words tumbled out in haste, rushing over each other. Maybe he wanted to say it, all of it, before he changed his mind—or rather, lost his courage. He'd seen the enticing ad displayed in the paper yesterday, and the festive imagery had grabbed his attention. He'd been interested—and even thought about going—before he quickly dismissed the idea.

It was crazy. He wasn't the type to go shopping or to enjoy the lights. He was too old for that kind of stuff. But Mary looked like she needed a good cheering up. And this was a good idea, a good thing to take her mind off of whatever was bothering her.

He was in the car and gripping the steering wheel before he realized it. He inhaled, sucking in air and then exhaling slowly. This seemed to relax his tight chest and loosen him up. He snuck a side glance at

Mary, who was looking out the passenger window, her arms crossed around her over the seat belt.

"You want more heat?" he asked.

She shook her head. "I'm bundled up. But you go ahead. Sometimes people ask when it's something they want to do. If you want to turn up the heat, I don't mind."

"The heater works great in this car." He fiddled with the dial, and his hand moved back to the steering wheel.

"How far are we?"

"About thirty minutes out. We should be there soon. You eager to get there?"

She let out a soft laugh. "No, time's what I've got. No... no hurry at all."

"We could tell stories."

"Oh yeah? Entertain me."

"Remember the time we had a contest in math class?"

"Wait... what was the teacher's name?"

"Ms. Elsa."

"Right." Mary clapped her hands. "I thought you didn't like math?"

"Math was one of the most boring classes, and it was easy to lose my focus," Brad said.

"Little Jimmy fell asleep and snored!" Mary squealed, chuckling with laughter.

"Ms. Elsa was so mad. She punished the entire class."

"I remember. On Fridays, she'd have a race to see

who could say the multiplication tables the fastest. Our weekly assignment was to learn one row or column, and at the end of the week, we had to recite it out loud, in front of the whole class. She'd randomly pick the students from folded slips of paper with each child's name inside a jar." Mary's eyes sparkled as she chatted enthusiastically.

"And the fastest kid to recite that week's multiplication row or column on the table would win a prize."

"I was praying my name wouldn't be called, even though Ms. Elsa said she had the coolest gifts. Two smart, nerdy kids sitting behind me sneered and boasted it'd be a piece of cake and they would win."

They drew five names that day in class. The first was one of the nerdy kids. Thin, with black-framed glasses and a slight stoop to his shoulders already. When Ms. Elsa called his name, he gave a whoop, shouting, "I know it." He smirked and straightened his shoulders as he stood up beside his desk.

Ms. Elsa had the stopwatch in one hand, ready to go. "Give me all the sixes," she had said, and counted down, "Three, two, one. Go."

Brad had listened to the kid spouting the numbers, almost garbling his words. He was overconfident, prematurely shining in his moment of expected victory.

Ms. Elsa wrote the time and picked up the plastic jar. The process started again. The next was a sandy-haired boy, then a girl in pigtails, followed by a chubby boy. Then the last slip of paper was drawn, and Ms. Elsa called out the name "Mary."

Brad was relieved his name hadn't been called. He knew his multiplication, but rattling it off in front of the class would've messed up his thinking. He shook his head, fixing his gaze on Mary when the teacher clicked the timer, noticing her poised stature. She spoke quietly and quickly, the numbers rolling off her tongue in a nonstop stream. Before he knew it, she had finished, and he heard the click of Ms. Elsa's thumb pushing down the stopper.

The class had waited in excited anticipation for the announcement, watching as the teacher wrote the final time, then picked up the sheet of paper and turned toward the class.

"We've had a close race today," Ms. Elsa said. "We had two people who clocked in at the same time."

The class grew quiet. Someone's chair skidded.

"However, one person made an error. One which they glossed over and kept on going." She paused and looked at the paper again, then announced, "The winner today, with all the correct answers, is Mary."

"You still remember," Mary said, breaking into his thoughts.

"You betcha." He grinned.

"Shucks, I'm surprised you brought it up."

"You know what those boys said after you beat them?"

"Which one... the what's his name, overconfident nerd?"

"Yep. He was a sore loser. Went back and argued with the teacher."

"Curious, though. What mistake did he make?"

"According to him, he didn't make one."

"Yeah, right!"

"And the teacher was wrong, so he says. Anyway, you beat him," Brad said.

"Funny you would bring it up now. It was over twenty years ago."

He leaned in. "I've always wondered... what was the prize you won?"

She laughed, sucking in air and almost choking. "Donuts."

"It was good, huh?"

"You know, Momma let me eat one for breakfast every day afterward. And one for dinner until it was all gone. I shared the donuts with them. She was so proud of me." Mary's voice broke, and she paused. "Dad was, too," she whispered.

"You miss him still?"

She nodded, looking away.

"I'm sorry. I know you two were close."

"He was a man of few words. Didn't believe in wasting breath on compliments."

"Don't expect any, and your feelings won't get hurt. I know what it's like to have expectations that don't amount to anything."

"I tried to be good, and I told him I'd do anything he asked. I didn't give him a hard time. But... in my heart, I knew Katie was his favorite."

"He shouldn't have said anything to you."

She shook her head. "No, he didn't say that to me. I overheard him talking to Momma once right before he died, and he was upset about something. Momma intervened and made the comment that Katie was his favorite. He didn't deny it or object."

"It's hurtful, isn't it?" Brad asked, his voice soft and empathetic.

She nodded. "He saw I was listening to their conversation and gestured to me with his hand to come closer."

"And?"

Mary swallowed, then smiled. "Then he whispered in my ear as I leaned in."

Brad saw the tear trickle down her cheek. He reached out and wiped it with the knuckle of his finger. He whispered, "What did your father say?"

"H-he said I'm the good daughter."

Her lips trembled and quivered.

Brad squeezed her hand and covered it with his. Sometimes, words didn't come easy, and this was one of those times. He felt her sadness, the grief inside, and how deeply those words meant to her, coming from her father to his daughter. Before he passed.

Her shoulders bent as sobs shook her body.

18

SHE HADN'T BEEN GOOD, MARY WANTED TO CONFESS TO her father. She coveted her sister's favored status and sought his approval. Mary was secretly delighted that she had made it to her father's deathbed, with her mother on one side and her on the other. For she had waited all her life for her father to recognize her and acknowledge her goodness. Yet, for all her wishful thinking, it had been left to God what a man or woman couldn't have control over. On his last day, her father's breathing was labored, and he fought to live, and then later, when he was tired and spent, he finally gave up and let go. It was inevitable.

The dying knew, she believed. It was what no doctor or anyone could predict. But those who were near death sometimes clung to life longer hoping to see or be with their loved ones. There was no comfort for lonely people dying in hospitals or in nursing homes, quarantined like prisoners on death row, separated from their loved ones, denied their last wish to see and be with them, denied one last touch, a kiss, a forever farewell as they left this earth.

Mary had, at the end of her father's life, wished what he wanted would come true as the time came for him to pass.

Momma and Mary had watched the man refuse food at the end and prepare for his own departure from this world. It was really the way he wanted to go, at home in his own bed, with his wife and daughter at his bedside, the last faces he'd see on Earth. And before he left this life, he'd given Mary his love and acknowledgment and praise as the good daughter. Those words she would never forget.

Momma had wept and cried her heart out; she was inconsolable at losing her first and only love. In that moment, Mary realized how deep and inseparable they had been. Her parents weren't the lovey-dovey kind, nor were they physically demonstrative in front of their children. It was rare to see them touch, and even rarer for them to kiss in front of her and Katie.

It ripped Mary's heart to see what death did to the person left behind. She saw firsthand the pain and anguish of the solitary heart. If she ever found a love so deep and strong, Mary vowed she'd want to be the first to go.

In a moment of vulnerability, she'd let herself open up and expose to Brad the rot at the core, and the hurt and unworthiness she carried in her being. She hadn't meant for it to happen. She'd hidden this secret pain for so long, all alone, and not shared with her mother, sister, or anyone.

Even with Jim, in her most private moments of revelations and murmurs, something had held her back. Was it her heart? Deep inside, she hadn't let go. She kept this part of herself hidden. Would Jim have cared for her then? Would Jim have been thoughtful, receptive, and non-judgmental? She didn't take the chance, and she knew she'd never share it with him.

But Brad—oh, how she opened up and ripped away the covering she'd hidden behind for so long. The aches, the shame, the guilt with her father.

What of Brad, especially after what she did to him, years ago in high school—would he forgive her?

Her cheeks reddened at the memory of that day, so long ago. She'd buried it, too. Bid it to disappear. But it had happened. She couldn't make the truth evaporate. It had started so innocently.

Mary bit her lip and glanced at Brad. Would he still remember? Should she bring it up and ask him? Maybe it was better to let it lie for now. Caught in these powerful emotions, her head and her heart pulled in separate ways. Wanting to apologize to Brad for a wrong she'd done years ago, or press her lips and stay silent. But she'd have to live with it.

19

BRAD FELT CONFLICTED, THINKING OF MARY'S BETRAYAL. She talked about her father and being the good daughter. But he knew she wasn't a good person, the way she treated him. Brad wanted Mary to beg him for forgiveness. He pursed his lips, holding back the words he wanted to mutter, knowing she couldn't hear. He wanted to forget the moment when she dealt the crushing blow to his tender heart. But he couldn't just yet. He still felt the pain and carried the scar. He practiced mumbling, moving his jaws just the tiniest bit. He choked on the words.

He had calmed her as she poured out her heart and sobbed until she was exhausted and spent.

He'd carried a wound for over ten years, keeping it safe in his beating heart. It was his secret and his hurt, for Mary had wronged him. So much so, he turned from her and from this town, vowing never to undergo that kind of hurt again. He remembered as clearly as if it happened yesterday.

That afternoon, they had gathered in front of the drugstore. It was one of their favorite spots, an after-school hangout. Brad and Jim had arrived first, and they sat on the wrought-iron bench in front of the store, facing the street. Laurie joined them shortly, followed by Mary, Katie, and Chase. They had congregated in their usual place, laughing and carrying on. It was senior year for most of them, and the conversation soon turned to the subject of the prom.

Brad had been getting up the nerve to ask Mary to go with him. But he hadn't yet. Mary had joked around. Maybe she wanted to prod him, or maybe she was clueless. In any event, it made him more stubborn than ever. His mouth would not open. The teasing had gotten a bit out of hand, and Mary's voice grew louder. It was then she crossed over the line with her actions.

He remembered every detail of that moment.

Mary had been charmingly flirtatious, smiling boldly at Brad. He heard her laugh, light and melodious. She had walked over to where he and Jim were sitting on the bench and stood looking down at him.

"I heard a rumor you're going to the prom." She leaned in, looking straight at him. "Hmm… who's the lucky girl?" Her luminous eyes seemed to dance with light as the curtains of her long lashes fluttered.

He didn't like being put on the spot and muttered a curse word under his breath, but loud enough that she could hear.

She laughed, louder that time. "I heard you want to go with me."

Brad gritted his teeth and pushed out a gruff sound.

She wouldn't stop. "A little bird told me you wanted to ask me..." The singsong lilt of her voice dropped and hesitated, wavering, as if unsure whether to finish the sentence with a dot at the end or a question mark. Her lips quivered.

He wanted to ask her in his way and to surprise her. This wasn't the way it should be. A part of him wanted to say yes, but another part was resistant. It was like a tug of war, his thoughts going this way and that.

He hesitated.

She put her hands on her hips, putting on a smile that stretched wide. But her eyes no longer danced.

Brad shifted his feet, buying more time. But he'd run out.

Mary was speaking again, her voice somehow odd, different. "Well, Jim's taking me to the prom, so you needn't bother." It sounded hollow, strange. She moved toward Jim, still sitting on the bench. In one fell swoop, she plopped on his lap and put her arms around his neck. "You are, aren't you?"

He could still see Jim's slightly dazed expression, mouth slack and frowning.

Then she kissed him, full on the mouth.

A growl emanated from Brad's throat, and emotion took over reason. Blood rushed to his cheeks and reddened it. He flexed his fingers and gripped his hand into a ball, wanting to punch Jim in the face, fueled by rage and humiliation. He watched helplessly as Jim returned her kiss and deepened it.

He cursed her reckless heart.

20
___

FOR AS LONG AS SHE COULD REMEMBER, MARY HAD HAD a secret crush on Brad. Going back to elementary school. But she was shy and didn't tell anyone. Any person, at least.

She poured her heart out in her diary, where all her secrets were kept. It felt safe there. And she could keep it all to herself. If she'd uttered her secret, then it'd lose the special sparkle. Mary kept it close to her heart and put it all down in ink on paper.

It was almost a certainty Brad was unaware of her crush, since she'd given no sign of or said anything to him. It would have changed things if she made it known to him, but she was not the kind of girl who'd take that step. No, she was the good daughter, the good girl. Not because she wanted to be, or because she had to be. It was just who she was. She didn't question that.

By the time senior year rolled around, it went fast.

Suddenly, it was almost time for the prom, the end-of-year activities, and graduation. Mary realized the last hurrah would come at last. Soon, Brad would be leaving. Thus, that afternoon in front of the store, it felt like —but wasn't like—old times, the group of them together. Friends among friends. This time it was different—laced with an urgency.

Mary hadn't planned on it, but a spark of rebellion had been brewing, and the ticking clock sounded louder. They'd joked and laughed and chilled out that afternoon in front of their favorite hangout spot on the sidewalk on Main Street. She had felt giddy, fueled by an inner boldness pushing her to action, to bring up the prom with Brad, to ask him the question her mind had circled around and around for days and weeks and months. She had hoped he'd ask her, of course. But as the time drew close, and he had not, she took it upon herself. It was out of character, surprising even her.

She'd used the light flirting to cover up her nervousness. Mary had pushed the words out in a playful tone. But he had not responded. She'd looked into his eyes, seeking the answer, and watched his mouth, waiting for words to tumble out.

When they didn't, her heart was wounded. It beat slower, retreating.

Then something seized her, and she did something reckless. Jim.

Mary landed on Jim's lap and wrapped her arms around him like it was the most natural thing in the world, as if she'd done it many times. She felt a high, a sense of boldness and daring—and before she could stop herself, her lips had met his.

She'd turned halfway around when she felt Brad's piercing eyes burn into her back. Mary had relished that initial euphoric moment, the fleeting sense of triumph and independence, the reckless abandon to the rest of the world.

It lasted not even a minute. There were no cheers, no congrats. Just silence. Shocked silence.

Mary had popped her eyelids wide open, taking a quick scan. Doing a head count. Yup, everyone was there.

Her eyes locked with Brad, taking in the disapproval and utter disgust in his eyes. And his body language sent another message, clearly delivered by the rounded shoulders and the resignation and disappointment of rejection. It was as clear as a football field after a game, the thunderous sound of winning contrasting with the silence of defeat. It was then she realized the consequence of her action, along with the awful sinking feeling of knowing she'd messed up really bad, and there was nothing she could do about it.

The relay of the message and the reply took all of a second or two. Her mind took over, and her body froze. All those years of scribbling in her journal and wanting and waiting for Brad had come to this—this one reckless moment—and Mary had no one to thank but herself.

There was no going back, no rewinding the time. No starting over. There was no going forward.

By the time she pulled away from Jim, Brad had left. He was gone.

Brad's cell phone buzzed with another text after they arrived at the market. He frowned, and a scowl appeared on his face. He had left explicit directions not to be disturbed this weekend. What part of "Do Not Disturb" did they not understand? He stepped away from Mary to check his messages. A quick scroll of his texts showed most of it came from one person— the person he'd left in charge. It was all the same messages: trying to reach him, important, call back, urgent.

With an impatient tap of his fingertip, he called back.

"This better be important," Brad said as soon as the call was picked up.

"Well, it's about time you called."

"I said I didn't want to be disturbed."

"No deal, it fell apart."

"Did you make a counteroffer?"

"Yes, up to your pre-approved amount. But they said no."

"Greedy bastards." Brad cursed.

"Maybe we can salvage it if you come back."

"I need to stay here another day." Brad paused and ran his fingers through his hair. "You take care of it. Go to Plan B."

"Yes, sir. I'll handle it."

Brad slid the phone into his pocket, making sure it was still on silent. He wasn't ready to return to the city. Not just yet. He had things to take care of down here, too. And Mary was at the top of his list.

All those years ago, Brad had been humiliated in front of his friends by the one person he thought he liked. One person whom he'd come out of his shell for. He'd let his heart crack open, not all the way, but wide enough. When things got tough in business, he'd persevere and keep on. He's gotten good at it, outlasting his competitors. He'd earned an excellent reputation with his employees. The boss who'd have their backs. He'd gained their loyalty and shown them they could trust him.

With Mary, she had slammed shut the crack in the door in his face—and without remorse. That day in front of the drugstore, she had thrown up her chin and belted out a long, throaty laugh as one arm languished over Jim's shoulder. She'd been heartless, even cruel, punishing him for something she wanted him to do. No, what she'd wanted to force him to do in front of their friends. And when Brad didn't capitulate, she'd lashed out. The laugh, though, had died quick as she realized what she'd done. As soon as she realized it wasn't funny, when she had sealed her fate—with Jim. With the kiss. And Jim was willing, quite willing. Most willing.

Brad remembered how she'd stiffened and gritted her teeth. The smile had died on her face, lopsided and crooked, her mouth hanging half-open. He wanted to grab her and shake her silly. Make her apologize to him.

He'd leaned in, anticipating an apology. But she did nothing. She just froze. Not a word came out.

That scene had replayed in Brad's mind many times, and he couldn't wipe it out. How he wished he could erase it. He'd pinned his hopes and dreams on the cusp of change, when goodbyes and teary eyes celebrated the completion of one phase, the end of high school, and the beginning of another phase in their lives, becoming an adult in the world. The last farewell at senior prom carried a special meaning in his heart. But it wasn't fulfilled.

It was really his fault for delaying, for not asking Mary sooner. It took courage. And he had chided himself to work up enough nerve to ask her. In retrospect, it shouldn't have been a big deal, but back then —to a young man facing the situation for the first time —it was a big deal.

It wasn't just Mary's rejection, but also his failure to act when he needed to. He'd learned a hard lesson then, one he'd never forgot. One he'd paid the price for, a heavy price still extracting payment from a heavy heart. Mary had acted to force an outcome. But she'd failed, for instead of the response she sought, Brad had done the opposite. He had simply accepted it and left Mary to her decision, which she lived with, too, for the next ten years.

Maybe he wanted to punish her for her reckless act. In the end, it backfired, because it was not only Mary who was punished by his childish, vengeful act, but he had been terribly injured himself, and quite possibly Jim, as well.

Brad blinked away the trickle of tears from the corner of his eyes. His lips felt dry. He flicked his tongue and licked a drop, tasting the salty liquid.

The sunlight streamed across the landscape at the new market square, decorated for the festive season and strung with holiday lights. He raised his face toward the sky, willing for the warmth and brightness to take away his pain and ease his sadness. He'd reached the point of the lowest of lows, the inner torment of love unrequited. The years had taken a toll on him. The thin boy was gone, replaced by a mature, handsome man. A man who'd put up a shield and closed his heart for so long. For what couldn't be reached couldn't be hurt.

Daring the sunlight to reach the abscess hidden deeply, he yearned for it to warm his heart, to open it. Maybe Mary would soothe his soul and heal his wounded heart. Maybe she'd take away the regrets and pain. Maybe she would. Maybe this time.

Brad felt a stirring, a thread of hope making its way up. He gripped his gloves so tightly, his knuckles turned white. It was time to find out. Either way, it was time to resolve this. He had his hope, and he'd clung to it. Yet his mind cautioned him. For he wasn't reckless. Could he give up caution and let it be this time?

22

MARY TOOK A DEEP BREATH AND EXHALED, SENDING THE
warm air into the frosty afternoon. She pulled her coat
tighter as a gust of wind blew. Off to the side, a few
steps away, Brad was still on the phone. She couldn't
hear what he was saying, but from his frown, she could
tell he wasn't enjoying the conversation.

Spending time together was almost like the old
days when they were friends and hung out. But being
close to Brad now, without a crowd, stirred emotions
she had buried.

She stole another sideways glance at him, studying
his profile. He was pacing now, his legs moving in
short, fast strides, impatient to be done with the call.
She couldn't take her eyes off this handsome man, and
the assured, confident way he moved. Mesmerized, she
watched his lips shape the sounds of words, fixating on
his mouth. An uncontrollable quiver ran through her
body. She longed for the touch of those lips. But these

weren't the inexperienced, adolescent lips of a shy teenager. These lips were manly, bold, and defined.

She lowered her lids, hiding the raw desire in her eyes. She let her imagination loose. She wanted him to want her, to chase her, to woo her. To come after her and beg her. No, not beg. Ask. She wanted to hear him say it, those words to her, to ask her to prom, to be his date for the biggest event in their senior year. What he didn't say ten years ago. She wanted him to say it now.

She shrugged, pulling herself back to her senses. Who was she fooling, anyway? The present was here and now. Mary stomped her feet on the snow, leaving the imprint of her shoes. She needed to stop the daydreaming and wishful thinking, which would get her nowhere.

She watched as Brad finished his conversation and slid the phone into his pocket. He had walked away to talk, but after the call ended, he stood there, legs planted on the ground, rubbing his face and running his hand through his hair. Why was he upset? She wondered. Impatiently, Mary hurried toward him, taking quick steps.

"Is everything all right?"

He looked up and scrutinized her face, as if searching for something. He sighed, speaking quietly. "I need to go back."

She gasped, taking a step back. "Y—you mean now?" Well, that sucked, she thought, as the film she played in her mind came to a screeching stop as the director yelled, "Cut!"

Brad shook his head. "Soon."

"S-s-soon?" she sputtered like an incoherent idiot.

"I've got business to take care of."

"Delegate it," she snapped.

He studied her face, and an amused smile crossed his lips. "Ma'am, you'd make a crackin' boss."

Mary blushed and hoped he didn't notice. "I mean… it's what I'd do if I had trusted people."

"You're right. I've got someone working on my Plan B."

She brightened at this bit of good news. "Great minds think alike," Mary said, giggling. "Seriously, what kind of problems are you facing?"

"I'm a builder," Brad said.

She acknowledged it with a nod.

"We've bought land in the city to build a tiny home community."

"Right, your project. I've seen cute tiny homes in magazines," Mary gushed enthusiastically. "They're adorable."

"And they'll leave a smaller carbon footprint. Our houses will be environmentally conscious, and we'll install energy-saving devices."

"Is that more affordable?"

"Housing prices and rentals have skyrocketed, and it's a struggle to find good, affordable housing with a yard, even if it's on a postage-sized piece of land."

Mary clutched her hand, envisioning a cluster of tiny houses with green space surrounding each. "Have you started building? What's your emergency?"

"Yes, we have, and there are deadlines to meet. Unfortunately, the costs have risen, and there are supply-chain issues for building materials and environmental items. We're seeing delays of several weeks or months on some orders."

"What can you do?"

"We're working on Plan B."

"You and the person on the phone?"

He nodded. "Kell."

Mary frowned. "Your right-hand man?"

"Woman. I believe you've met her."

"Umm... I think you have me confused with someone else." Mary hesitated. "Where would I have met her?"

"At Laurie's wedding. The blonde I was with," Brad said.

Mary felt her cheeks burn. She remembered. The beautiful, sophisticated blonde. She'd turned everyone's heads. Mary worked her mouth and cleared her throat. "Th—that's Kell? Your wedding date? And she's working with you on your Plan B?"

She quickly recovered from her fumbling as he smiled and nodded. "I know you're a businessman, but what you're doing is so much more. You're building a dream for city dwellers, where they can enjoy living in an urban area, but in a tiny house community where it's affordable." She paused. "And it's also fun and super cool."

"Well, you're going to have to come see it when it's

done." He raised an eyebrow, waiting to see her response.

"I can't wait," Mary said. "I accept your invite." She threw up her arms and leaned in for a hug. A quick, spontaneous one. Except it wasn't quite so quick.

23

———

BRAD HUGGED HER TIGHT, WRAPPING HIS ARMS AROUND Mary and resting his head on her shoulder, burying his face amongst the long strands of her hair. He nuzzled his nose in the thick locks, inhaling the pleasant scent and closing his eyes. The big city seemed so far away now. He had another life, a hectic one filled with meetings, schedules, and deadlines. He'd abandoned the small town where he grew up, just like he'd abandoned any hopes of going to the prom with Mary. It was not a big deal now. But back then, in another time and place, it had been a big deal.

"It'll work out. You can do it," Mary was saying.

Brad didn't tell her about his worries and the challenges in pulling off this new project. He was determined not to raise the price of the tiny houses, even as material costs increased. He took pride in his company, and in not taking shortcuts when other companies were doing it. People rarely inquired about hidden things they couldn't see, like studs, when they purchased a home. The house he grew up in had studs spaced twelve inches apart. Now, companies were building houses with wall studs sixteen inches apart, and in some new houses, twenty-four inches apart. Builders cut costs with differences in materials, design, and construction. They didn't build houses the way they used to, that was for sure.

Brad was determined not to take shortcuts in the tiny houses. It was a sense of pride, and doing the right thing meant a lot to him.

Mary's eyes were glowing with admiration. He knew she believed in him and in the work he was doing. And to be honest, a part of him wanted to hear her say this. It mattered to him.

He couldn't believe this starry-eyed girl—no, not a girl anymore, this woman—was the same person who had humiliated him ten years earlier. Did she know then what had mattered to him? Would this glow in her eyes be so easily turned on, then off, as it had years ago? Brad remembered it like it had happened yesterday. The quick change in her affection, from one guy to another. The flirty teasing she'd flattered him with, and he had naively believed Mary was actually interested in him. He wasn't so quick then to exchange witty comebacks or to return flattery. He remembered the come-hither look she'd given him, the pout on her lips, and the attention thrown in his direction—was it for real or playacting?

But Brad wasn't that kind of guy. Not back then.

And she hadn't been that kind of girl, not the one he'd known since grade school. It was out of character for her. He didn't like the change in her then, nor did he understand why or how it happened. The easy banter between them, familiar amongst friends, was gone. Instead, appearing before him was a coquettish, flirty woman who batted her lashes and tossed lines at him. He didn't take her up on it. Not right away, for it was his nature to think things through, toss it around in his mind, and mull it over before he decided.

Clearly, he wasn't the guy for her then. In less than a minute, he'd gone from being the object of affection and attention to, well, a cast-off. As easily replaceable as a discarded napkin.

His heartbeat quickened as his memories were dragged up, that sliver in time pulled out. How well did he really know Mary? People said some things never changed. In the years since he'd moved away, they'd not kept in touch. What was the point? Brad had heard she was dating Jim, and it was getting pretty serious. Eventually, he'd pushed her out of his mind and closed the book on it.

"Hello, anyone home?" Mary was playfully knocking on his temple. "Knock, knock."

"Who's there?" he responded, catching on to her game.

"Mary."

"Mary who?"

"Marry me." She smiled and grabbed his hand, the

left one, turning it front to back, pretending to look for a ring. "Um… you don't have a ring."

He pulled her hand into his and twined their fingers together. "It's my turn."

She raised an eyebrow.

He lifted his finger and touched her cheek. Then he tilted her head until her lips were upturned. "Kiss me," Brad murmured, his warm breath a prelude to what he'd offer. He looked her in the eye, boldly exclaiming his desire for her to see as he mustered every ounce of strength to hold back.

She responded, her eyes full of longing.

He didn't wait another second. His lips crushed hers, sucking her mouth, taking it for all he was worth, claiming his right. Finally.

She pressed against him, her breathing erratic and rushed, hungrily giving him what he wanted and taking what she needed. She was greedy, wanting him as much as he wanted her.

Brad waved all logic aside and surrendered to the moment. The kiss he'd been waiting for all these years. It was what he'd imagined. No, scratch that. It was nothing like he'd imagined. Gone was the timid Mary and her clumsy attempts to beguile him.

Now she was a red-blooded, sexy woman who was sure of herself and knew what she wanted.

Maybe he was making up for lost time. Maybe she was, too. Brad didn't care. He was lost in the moment as his wildest dreams came true. The kiss was the longest wet dream he ever had. When he opened his eyes,

Mary was still there in his arms. She had the widest grin on her face, and her lipstick was smeared.

He reached up with his thumb to rub off the areas smudged with lipstick, concentrating on the task at hand. Her skin was soft, sprinkled with scattered freckles. He took his time to wipe off the smeared pink color.

"There, all good," he said when he was done.

24

———

Mary woke up late, having fallen into a deep sleep the night before. She rubbed her eyes and yawned, stretching her arms wide. She smiled, vaguely remembering the sweet dreams that all featured Brad in them.

Spending most of the day with him yesterday had been more than she could have asked for. He was such a gentleman. He'd shown his appreciation by taking her to dinner at an out-of-town place, a rather fancy restaurant. They'd shared appetizers, and stretched the three-course meal into over two hours. At one point, the server hovered over them a tad bit too long. Of course, Brad took the hint and acknowledged it, and rewarded him with a generous tip.

Mary remembered how they'd talked easily, laughing often, their words flowing as smoothly as the rich, fine wine. They'd tarried, reluctant to leave. By the time they had consumed the meal, she barely had room for dessert. They shared one slice of decadent dark chocolate cake. She made room for this, lifting her fork to her mouth, loaded with the final, moist bite. She'd licked her lips, savoring the rich taste and the creamy frosting. The food was delicious, but the company was the best part. She'd gazed into Brad's eyes, and hung on to every word. Acting like a silly, love-struck young girl. Oh, but wait. She was an almost thirty-year-old woman, forgetting how old she was and thoroughly enjoying it.

It'd been a fun-filled day with light-hearted laughs and lingering holiday cheer. Squeezing in the last hours of the New Year's long weekend.

When they parted, Brad was smiling, but it didn't quite reach his eyes. Mary had locked eyes with him, but his were lukewarm and missing the sparkle she'd seen throughout the day. It wasn't the kiss good night that was the problem. The man who kissed her had been so patient. His kiss passionate but not rushed. She felt her face flush, remembering his touch and the pressure of his lips. No, it was something else troubling him. Maybe it had to do with the call.

She'd asked him about it, seeing the worry on his face.

He'd turned and looked at her square in her face, and told her not to worry. He said he'd handle it, but didn't go into details about it.

Mary had taken him at his word and didn't probe further. She wasn't the sort of girl to nag. If she told him once, and the words were out of her mouth, she considered it done. Then whatever Brad did was his decision. For what it was worth, once it left her mind, she'd most likely forget it and wipe her hands clean. She wasn't the type to keep after a guy, wearing him down until he gave in, as some girls did. The word "nag" would not be in her vocabulary. What she wanted in a man was a strong one.

Wordlessly, she had reached out her hand, placing it over his large ones. She'd left it there, then squeezed him. What she didn't say was communicated by her gesture. It was what she'd do to comfort an old friend when words seemed inadequate, or the right ones wouldn't come to mind.

He'd leaned in, turning and lifting his hand to meet hers palm to palm, then covered hers on top with his other hand, like a sandwich.

She felt the warmth of his touch and the response. Brad had received her message and let her know he had her covered. There was a glint of gratitude in his eyes.

"I have to go back," he said. "Take care of things."

She'd frowned and mumbled, "I don't understand. Didn't you tell your people to go to Plan B?"

"I did."

"What's the problem?"

He'd shaken his head.

"What is it you're not telling me?" Mary had blurted out.

"It... it's worse than I thought. I got another call."

Mary couldn't hide the disappointment on her face.

She figured it must've been pretty bad for Brad to be so worried.

He'd squeezed her hand and bent his head, whispering in her ear, "Sleep well tonight. Tomorrow's another day."

She had searched his face, looking for another response. All she saw was the tiredness in his eyes and the puffiness underneath. The lines on his face had deepened.

"You sleep on it. Maybe an answer will pop out in your dreams before tomorrow morning. Sometimes it happens to me when I least expect it, like when I'm in the shower, brushing my teeth," Mary said, putting a smile on her face.

25

IT HAD BEEN A PERFECT DAY. BRAD HAD IGNORED HIS calls until the incessant ringing irritated him. Why couldn't he have one day with Mary, undisturbed? He'd given strict orders at work not to be bothered this weekend. And no one else would have dared—except for Kell, the icy blonde who had a thing for him. He should've fired her then, but regretting it now would not change anything.

Kell had no scruples in love or work. Her competitive nature was to win, at any cost. Even now, Brad grudgingly admitted she had balls, more than any man in his company. She could kick ass and had no qualms about doing so. She'd played him in the beginning, leading him to believe that together as a team, they'd be a winning combination. That was until she'd overstepped.

He knew better than to trust her again. But she knew exactly where and when and how to push his buttons and manipulate him. She'd pushed him to the limit more than once, and left him seething in anger. Her call infuriated him, upset him. Kell seemed to take delight in it, wielding the power she had, what was left of it after it had deflated to an all-time low. But it didn't have to be this way. They had sat down together and talked. He'd taken the opportunity to inform her how things would be from then on. He'd reined her in and kept a tight leash on her, giving her one more chance. Brad was explicitly clear and didn't mince words. She knew what the stakes were this time.

Getting involved with Kell personally was a mistake, and he'd regretted it afterward. It wasn't planned. At least not by him. He remembered how it started. He'd been working late at the office, absorbed in plans, when she'd knocked on his door and walked in without waiting for his response.

It was late, and the time had slipped his mind. Kell was on her way out and asked if Brad wanted anything before she left. He'd said jokingly, oh yeah, if she could bring him a steak. She'd swayed, leaning against the door, and suggested they grab a bite together. He'd turned her down and said he wanted to finish what he was working on tonight. But then his stomach grumbled. He'd laughed and thought it funny his body made sounds as if on cue.

He'd sat back and swiveled in his expensive, sleek black chair, a reflex action, twirling around.

Kell had walked up to him and lifted her leg to stop

the momentum of the chair, her dress pulling up on her thighs.

He'd gulped, taken by surprise. It took her about a second to make the next move as she slithered across his body, her arms extended, and her hands fumbled to unbutton his shirt and loosen his tie. He was boxed in, butt stuck in his chair, while she made the moves. Brad attempted to reject her advances. That was, until she planted a kiss, smothering his words as her tongue shoved deep into his throat.

One thing led to another, and although his mind was sending red alerts and warnings of the improprieties, his body hardened, disregarding those thoughts. He froze, pressing his head back against the headrest of the chair while images of a female praying mantis attacking its mate, looming over it and pinning it down before sucking the life out of the male, played in his mind. It was all he could think of in that state.

He had gulped as he saw the triumphant look in her eyes. Heard her breathing quicken. Felt the weight of her body and the power and excitement fueling her aggression. He knew if he gave in, he'd be a goner. It'd be quick, but when it was over, he'd forever be in her clutches. His mind processed this in a matter of seconds. Then he fought her, taking back his space, regaining ground, all the while gripping the belt buckle of his pants.

A high-pitched noise had jolted him back to reality, as the night custodian turned on the vacuum cleaner and started cleaning the hallway floor.

Kell stood up, but not before turning around and grinding her butt hard against his lap. Then she pulled down her dress. Brad buttoned up his shirt and straightened his tie. The noise of the vacuum cleaner grew louder. They hurried and walked out of the office, Kell first. Brad kept a distance behind, nodding to the night custodian as he passed, then took the elevator down to the first floor. They parted ways, dinner forgotten.

There wasn't any way to undo what had happened. Brad had gone home that night, taken a long, steamy shower, and went to bed, exhausted. He didn't want to think about tomorrow, or the next day, what he'd say to her. It was against office policy. For sure. And she knew it. He should've known better.

The next morning, he dressed carefully. Part of him was torn about seeing Kell in the office, wondering how he'd react. How she'd react. Would she pretend everything was normal? Or would she touch him or do things to remind him they had kissed in his office? Would she tease him again and press him for more?

He'd convinced himself with a stern self-talk that he had to set the stage for behavior at work and put an end to this... what would he call it? This one-time thing? Admittedly, Brad found her attractive. Thinking back, he recalled the time he'd been in a bind before when he needed a plus one to attend Laurie's wedding. He didn't have a girlfriend then and needed a pretend plus one, and it had slipped out at work when he was discussing his schedule with Kell. She jumped on the opportunity and said she would accompany him as his fake plus one.

In the daylight, he wondered if what happened last night truly happened. He shook his head, like freeing himself from a spider trying to trap him, unraveling from her silken strings.

He read Kell the riot act in the morning. It was the first thing he did when she came into the office. The ice queen had been a fitting title for her, and he'd put a crack in it.

The sound of an incoming call brought Brad back to the present day. He picked up his cell. He had chosen a special ringtone just for Mary. After the second ring, he pressed the answer button.

"Hi."

"How are you this morning? Did you sleep well?" she asked.

"I got about five hours in. It could have been better, but I'm not complaining."

"I had a great time yesterday. And thank you for the wonderful dinner."

"Hey, I'm just glad you had fun." He chuckled. "And it got me out of work."

"You know what they say about Jack... all work and no play."

Brad laughed, his eyes crinkling, though Mary wasn't there to see it. "I should come back more often."

"You should," she repeated, a bit emphatically. Then she paused. "So... are you leaving today?"

"On my way out."

Mary was quiet on the other end.

"Would you like to say goodbye… in person?" she mumbled.

Brad hesitated. He had a lot on his plate, and he hadn't intended to see her again before he left town.

"Can we meet for coffee?" Mary asked, pressing for an answer.

Brad paused, checking the time. "When? I'm packed and ready to go."

"I can be out the door now."

"Let's make it quick. Where to?"

"Oh, I know just the place. It's a cute little coffee shop with a few breakfast items in the cooler. Casual and unpretentious décor. I love it."

"Text me the address. I'll meet you there."

"Okay."

Brad smiled. Maybe seeing Mary again wasn't such a bad thing to do on his way out. The sun seemed brighter and the sky bluer. Yesterday's worries were behind him. For now. He was determined to enjoy the morning.

26

Mary was the first one to arrive at the Morning Glow Café. She hurried in, scanning the place for a good table. She nodded, pleased her usual spot was available.

The waitress smiled in recognition and grabbed two menus and tableware settings rolled in napkins when Mary held up two fingers. She quickly seated Mary and brought out two glasses of water.

"Thank you." Mary leaned back on the chair and took a sip of the ice water. The ambiance was cozy and charming. The tall windows stretched high, giving plenty of openings for the sunshine to brighten up the room. The structure was well-built, with wood ceilings, walls, and floors throughout. It was solid, good wood that had lasted over two decades, with scratches and dents to mark the time and show age. Countless people had trodden on the planks and sat on well-worn seats.

She loved coming here. The clinking of utensils, soft-spoken conversations, and occasional laughter were relaxing sounds to her ears. Most times, Mary would order coffee and a pastry or hard-boiled eggs, and bring a book to read. It was a treat she allowed herself, one she looked forward to at least once a week. The waitresses all knew her, and she was a regular at the establishment.

The thought of Brad's kiss brought a shy smile. It was every bit as she'd dreamed. Some people might think it was foolhardy to hold on to dreams, and for so long. But she didn't care. She never lost hope. She got what she dreamed of, and it was worth it. So very well worth every second of it. She giggled, the laughter of a once-shy teenager slipping out. It was happiness dancing in her heart, and she released it to the world to be heard. To be celebrated.

Some people were unbelievers, scoffing at even the idea of waiting for ten years. They'd laugh at it, ridiculing the person who carried memories from years ago. That was one reason Mary kept her feelings close to her heart, like a pure treasure to be cherished, for as long as her memories stayed with her. One never forgot their first puppy love. It was sweetness, innocence, and secret longing that ached. Mary had wondered if that would be a part of love, too. It was both a source of joy and pain.

When she saw Brad, the familiar butterflies flittered, and her heart quickened its beat on autopilot, just like every time.

"Hey," he said, walking up to her chair. "Been waiting long?"

"No, I just got here."

He bent over and kissed her cheek in greeting. "You smell nice." He grinned.

"You look nice." Mary glanced at the stylish outfit he'd thrown together in a casual, chic way. She could never do it, lacking the artistic talent to make it look so effortless. She was dressed in a navy sweater and jeans. Plain and basic.

The waitress came by, and they quickly ordered. Two coffees, and a slice of quiche for Mary and a breakfast sandwich for Brad.

The morning crowd was still thin. It was pleasant, the best time to come. Mary's favorite place, at her favorite table, with Brad. What more could she ask for? Blessings came in all sizes, and this was one. Mary said a quick thank you to God, whispering it. Bring on the day.

Their coffees and food came. She sipped her drink cautiously, testing the temperature, and inhaling the aroma of her favorite blend. Satisfied, Mary set the mug down and smiled. The Brad sitting across the table was a sight to see. She had the urge to run her fingers through his unruly, thick hair and touch the loose strand hanging in the way. He was one of those men who looked better as they aged. Her heart panged at the thought of having missed all those years with him. But he wasn't hers then.

This was how she imagined it, starting the day with

someone you loved over coffee and breakfast. She'd wanted that. She'd wanted him. And when he left—she'd miss him again. She took a deep breath, then picked up her mug.

"I can see why this is your favorite place," Brad said, breaking into her thoughts.

"I love coming here. Sometimes I bring a book to read and have coffee and a pastry or sandwich. It's great to relax, and a treat for myself."

He nodded. "It's the simple things in life that bring the most joy sometimes."

"Yes, and sometimes the unexpected, least of all when you're not looking for it."

"Coincidences also," he added. "You never know what life will bring your way."

And what about goodbyes? Mary thought sadly. She couldn't bring herself to verbalize it. Didn't trust herself to say those words. As if voicing it would make it final. Today, Brad would be gone again, back to the city. She wouldn't trade this weekend for anything. The time spent with him had been worth every minute.

She'd lived with the pain and paid the price for her recklessness. The past was done, over with. This moment, right now, he was sitting here in flesh and blood. Mary took a mental snapshot of him across the table from her. She wanted to capture this moment forever, or better yet, have a lifetime of morning coffees with Brad. For her, the wait had been worthwhile. Every bit of pain and heartache had led to this.

She swallowed, holding back the ache in her chest.

She wanted to say, "Wait, we didn't have enough time." Her mouth twisted, shaping and reshaping the words.

Brad reached for his cell phone and checked the display. "It's time."

She wondered if he could hear the frantic beating of her heart. The unuttered words caught in her throat. How she felt. But she was tongue-tied as a sinking feeling in the pit of her stomach weighed her down.

"I—I've enjoyed this weekend." She managed a smile, curving her lip.

She looked into his eyes, and their gazes held. A spark of something was exchanged. There was no confusion about it. This time, she was the one to pull away. But she couldn't just leave it hanging, this unspeakable thing between them. She had acted impulsively ten years ago. It wasn't a deliberate act to hurt Brad, yet she could see how he'd still be nursing it, a wound to his pride. A wound she'd inflicted thoughtlessly, recklessly.

His eyes held no anger now, but maybe a glint of resentment and sadness. He grabbed her hand and squeezed it. "I have to go."

"I never said I'm sorry before."

He shook his head and put a finger to her lips.

She gently grasped his finger. "I've thought of you as my friend first and foremost, ever since we were little kids. Remember the time when I climbed the monkey bars? In elementary school, on the playground? And that boy."

He frowned, then his face lit. "Right, and there was that kid."

"I can still see his face, his missing-toothed mouth and grin."

"Wonder what he's doing now—is he still here?"

"He never left. He's working at the ice cream store." Brad clenched his fist.

"It's not worth it now." She smiled, assuring him. "You took care of him then."

"The creep—how dare he look under your skirt." Brad worked his fist, clenching and unclenching it.

"You always watched out for me. So quiet, sometimes I didn't even know what you were doing."

"And look at you now. You've been taking care of yourself, and your father and your mother through the years."

"H-how did you know, before we talked?"

He grinned sheepishly. "Laurie's filled me in." He quickly added, "No, I wasn't asking about you, but sometimes when your name came up in our conversation, I'd casually ask. I wanted to know."

"Oh," Mary muttered as her cheeks flushed.

"She's well-intentioned."

"You know her as well as I do. She *loves* it. Nothing much slips by Laurie. She's got this radar thing, always has a feeler out."

"What I know is Laurie has a kind heart. She's our age, but she acts like a helicopter mom." Brad laughed and sputtered, coughing fluid that went down the wrong tube.

"I, for one, can't wait to see her as a mom. Maybe a baby will take all her attention."

"Hmm… imagine the poor kid growing up like that. I wouldn't want a mom who knew everything I did."

"Her kid will know love, too. Laurie doesn't have an evil bone in her body. She's protective, and her baby will be well cared for."

"No argument there," Brad said, his eyes crinkling.

Mary watched the smile lines deepen as they reached his eyes. She wondered what Brad would be like as a dad.

"And what about you?" Mary asked with a flirtatious laugh.

"What about me?"

"Do you want kids? A family? Why haven't you married?"

Mary noticed a change in his face—his smile had disappeared. His eyes turned aloof, with a glint of hardness that wasn't there before.

"I'm not putting the cart before the horse by making those plans now before I even have the right girl," Brad said, sounding testy as he snapped back a reply. Then he abruptly stood up from his chair and turned to leave.

27

———

IT WAS EVENING WHEN BRAD GOT BACK TO THE CITY. THE conversation with Mary had soured when he realized why she wanted to see him. He wasn't ready to talk about having kids and a family. She'd put a wrench in an otherwise fun weekend. He resented her asking. He resented her behavior ten years ago before the prom. He resented her now.

Brad pinched his mouth, seething with bitterness and anger inside. She had made her choice and chosen Jim ten years ago, and had been with him since. And now, after one weekend with Brad, she was asking *him* about kids? Was that her way of making a conciliatory effort? By putting him on the spot?

He wanted to be alone tonight. His place would be empty. Not even a cat waited for him. He was lucky to have stumbled on it. Rather, it was the real estate agent who had found it, minutes after the listing came live. It was in an ideal location and ticked off most of the boxes he had checked, which the agent had paid attention to when they discussed it. The day she drove him to see this place, it was love at first sight. It captured the image he'd had in his mind. He made an offer on it the same day; although it was a bit pricey, he went above it to beat out the competition. Anything to sweeten the deal. He was thrilled when the offer was accepted.

Brad parked in the expansive circular driveway and walked up to the front door. It was the elegant, dark wood door that caught his attention and made the first impression.

"Welcome home," he said as he walked in and dropped his keys on the hall table. His voice echoed in the empty house. He didn't expect a reply, and for a moment, he almost wished for a cat or dog to greet him. He shook his head. He'd make a lousy pet owner, with his busy lifestyle and demanding schedule. It wasn't the right time.

He took off his outer coat and hung it on the rack. A solitary hook held it. The other hooks were unoccupied. His views had shifted, the consciousness now on his aloneness, the emptiness of the house, taking in everything he hadn't given a thought to before. Moving through the house, he looked around as if he were newly discovering each room, making assessments and noting its bareness and potential.

It was a beautiful house, a mixture of modern sleek and cozy warmth. He hadn't expected to find it so easily, but he knew it was what he wanted as soon as he saw it. This home had character, and a freshness coupled with a feeling of warmth and charm that appealed to him. It was welcoming and accepting. He needed it, especially after a hard day at work.

The shrill ring of his cell startled him.

Kell's name popped up.

"Hey, what's up?" he answered.

"Are you home?"

The same old Kell, right to business.

"I just walked in the door."

"Have you checked your emails?"

"Look, I'll call you later," he said firmly before ending the call.

Brad loosened his tie and walked into the kitchen. He opened the refrigerator, but its contents were sparse—a half jug of juice, a carton of eggs, some cheese, and a stalk of limp celery. He surveyed the items in the pantry and decided on a can of chili. With a throbbing headache, cooking was the last thing on his mind. He could handle heating a can of soup, and it was just enough to assuage his hunger.

He had lost weight by eating light portions and cutting back on pasta, bread, and fried foods. Brad kept in shape, and his weight was only a few pounds more than he weighed in high school. His body was fuller now, but lean and muscled.

He moved smoothly and confidently, without insecurity or the need to fluff himself up or to raise his voice. Women and men knew instantly when he walked into a room. He was a natural, and a head-turner. Brad knew women drooled over him, and other men instinctively drew their arms around their wives or girlfriends. Yet he didn't pursue those women. It wasn't because he wasn't interested. He was a red-blooded American male. But he put up a screen and retreated behind it, which made women even more curious and determined to break the barrier and get to him. He didn't have to lift a finger, and they'd come. Tall women, short women, all kinds. He'd lost count of how many women. But he'd never lost his heart.

As he poured the chili into a bowl and warmed it in the microwave, he relaxed. He was glad to be back in his home. When the microwave beeped, he took the chili out and dug a spoon in it. That was easy. He was a bachelor and there were benefits to doing what he wanted, when he wanted, with no one to question him or to change the way he lived. He sighed, smiling as he brought the next spoonful to his lips.

28

THE FIRST TWENTY-FOUR HOURS WERE THE HARDEST, and time slowed down to a crawl. Every time the phone rang, Mary's heart skipped a beat, an anticipatory moment when she imagined the caller was Brad. Yet, again and again, she was disappointed. Time crept slower than molasses in those first days, then a week passed, then another and another, until a month had passed. Eventually, she assigned a special ringtone to his number, and it was still silent.

Mary had tried to stay busy in January. Anything to take her mind off Brad.

Things fell back into place. Momma had permanently moved into Chase and Katie's new home and helped to take care of Timmy. The weekly Sunday dinners were held at their house now.

On the last Sunday in February, after dessert and coffee had been served, Katie said she had an announcement to make. Mary noticed a glow on her sister's beaming face. Katie pushed back her chair and stood up, clasping her hands to her chest. When she had everyone's attention, barely able to contain her excitement, she let out the news: She and Chase were going to become parents. Exclamations of delight and squeals of joy erupted around the table, along with congratulations. The talk turned to excited chatter.

"Do you know the baby's sex?" Mary had asked.

"It's too early," her sister replied, explaining that when the time came to do the ultrasound, they would decide whether they wanted to know if it was a boy or girl or wait to be surprised.

Mary spent more time helping out at her sister's place during March. The expectant parents were knee-deep in preparations, even though it would be months before the baby arrived. There were so many things to do to prepare. Katie had found a doctor, and Chase went with his wife on her visits. Later, Katie confided to Mary that he was more excited than she was, if anyone could be, and he'd be an involved husband, by her side for every doctor visit and the birthing classes.

They turned the spare bedroom into a nursery and ordered a crib, mattress, sheets, changing table and dresser combination, and a baby bouncer to start, and made a list of other items to get. Katie was in charge of decorating the room and made trips to the stores to pick out colors and shop for baby clothes and other things for infants. She took Momma with her, leaving Mary to babysit Timmy when she came to help out.

She enjoyed being with Timmy. He had abundant

energy. Whenever they went outside to play, weather permitting, he exuberantly showed how fast he could run. She had to chase after him, leaving her panting and out of breath. A sign she was out of shape.

She wondered if she would have a family of her own someday. Mary was happy for her sister, and sharing her joy was infectious. A thought slipped into her mind that she was an intruder, an outsider looking in, and a feeling of sadness crossed fleetingly. She shook her head, determined to shrug off these thoughts. She was in charge of her life, and the decisions she'd made in the past, she couldn't change. The only path was forward, and Mary firmly fixed her feet to march on.

When Mary came back to her place and went to bed at night, she thought about Brad and wondered if he'd resolved the problems at work. She remembered the suave, handsome man who had come to Laurie's reception dinner with the strikingly beautiful and glamorous blonde. Mary couldn't help but notice the attention she'd attracted. She had claimed Brad and clung to him possessively in a familiar way, signaling they were more than friends. She wondered if the woman had reclaimed him again.

THE PHONE RANG. Mary glanced at her cell. She wasn't expecting any calls. She saw Laurie's name.

"Hey," she answered.

"Oh, is this a good time?" Laurie said.

"Yeah. Is—is something wrong?"

"It's, well…" She paused.

Mary could hear Laurie let out a sigh.

"Look, I thought you might want to know I just talked to Brad."

Heartbeat quickening, Mary gripped the phone. Her worst fears rose, and frenzied thoughts jumped into her head. What if something horrible had happened?

"Is he…?"

"He's been injured."

"Brad?" Mary said, her voice shaky. "How did it happen?"

"Construction accident."

Mary sucked in her breath. "Oh no. The last time I talked to him before he left, he… he was building the tiny homes…" Her voice trailed off. Anger reddened her cheeks. Brad had not called her since, and now he called Laurie? "Why did he call you?" she asked briskly.

"He didn't. I called him."

"Because?"

"I keep in touch with him."

She knew Laurie was like the social director of their group of friends. Even when they were kids, she liked to do this sort of thing, and matchmaking was second nature to her. But it hadn't occurred to her how often Brad and Laurie kept in touch outside of the occasional weddings and other celebratory invites that included Brad, along with the others in their group. She could kick herself for letting it slip out that she hadn't talked to him. But Laurie had.

"And how's he been?" Mary asked nonchalantly, keeping her voice on an even keel.

"He's been working hard to build the tiny houses. It's been a constant struggle to juggle materials and labor, and to run a tight schedule. I don't think the man sleeps more than four or five hours a day."

Mary pinched her lips, feeling ashamed and wiping away the images of Brad with the blonde woman, the two of them in a passionate embrace. Interesting, though, that her thoughts never went beyond this point. They'd stop before it got any further.

"Is he going to be all right?"

"I hope so. He's at the hospital. I think he's going to have surgery... or some procedure. It was hard to hear him clearly with the background noise. He couldn't talk long, and I didn't want to keep him on the phone."

Mary hadn't confided in anyone about her crush on Brad when they were younger. Even now, the sound of someone mentioning his name left her heart beating faster and her breathing shallow. She coughed to hide her reaction and quickly recovered. All she could think of saying was, "Why are you calling me?"

"I thought it was something you'd want to know," Laurie whispered, as if she was sharing a secret.

29

BRAD HAD BEEN PUSHING HIMSELF AND THE CREW TO meet deadlines. The challenge was to work around the delays and shortage of building materials and supplies. He'd spent countless hours in creative problem-solving and rescheduled parts of the projects while waiting for orders to come in. He'd contacted countless suppliers in order to find those who could fulfill the order or fill it faster.

Brad had no control over the weather, which contributed to delays and rescheduling. It'd been stressful dealing with supply-chain issues and the rising costs. He took care of his crew, paying them when labor costs increased while dealing with budget overruns and unexpected costs because of unforeseen circumstances and mistakes.

Prices had risen for gas, food, the cost of living. Everything was going in one direction only—up. It had been a seller's market when the interest rates had fallen to new lows, but with the rise in rates, that was no longer the case. First-time homebuyers hoping to qualify for mortgages found they could afford less house than they dreamed of. Even starter homes came with higher price tags.

Luckily for the tiny house market, it was still more affordable to singles, young couples starting out, and older couples who were downsizing and no longer needed the extra bedrooms and space after their children had moved out. Seniors on fixed incomes kept watchful eyes on their dwindling 401(k)s. For some, it made the difference between living comfortably in a tiny house versus having to scrimp and save to afford a larger home. For others, it was a lifestyle change for the minimalist at heart.

In the months since he'd gone back to the city, Brad buried himself in work. It kept his mind busy and occupied. But in the quiet moments when he was in the shower, or when he lay awake at night and couldn't fall asleep, he thought of Mary. The last time they had coffee in the café, it had been troubling. But he made sure he gave no promises or words of encouragement or plans for the future. He hadn't contacted her, and he couldn't really blame her for not contacting him. The distance he placed between them was in miles and more.

He remembered their kiss. Played the scene over and over in his mind. How could he forget her scent, the softness of her lips, the readiness and eagerness? Yet the one thing they'd never talked about was that day in high school, when she'd publicly humiliated him in front of their friends. He was young and inexperienced with women, and sensitive then, and she had played with his feelings and stomped on his tender heart. Worse, she had the audacity to flaunt a kiss with Jim, to top off the travesty.

The door flung open, and a nurse walked in to check on the patient on the hospital bed.

Brad's eyes moved from the man lying on the bed back to the nurse and held her gaze. He recognized her, a motherly woman with strands of out-of-place gray hair and a friendly face, and smiled.

She adjusted the man's bed.

"How is Cody?"

The nurse flipped his chart, scanning the pages. "He's on pain meds after foot surgery. Doctor is keeping him on observation overnight." Raising her head, she glanced at Brad. Her voice softened. "He's resting now. You're still here. Have you eaten dinner?"

He shook his head. "Not yet."

"The cafeteria is closed now. Why don't you go home?"

"Cody—"

"He's sleeping. You get some rest, too, and come back tomorrow."

Brad felt weariness descend like a heavy cloak. His eyelids drooped. He stifled a yawn.

"Yeah, I'll go home."

He glanced at Cody, his eyes shut tight, and watched the gentle rise and fall of his chest. Brad felt a twinge of guilt at pushing the crew to work long hours, though he paid overtime for those who did. Some men needed the money and volunteered for double shifts. Cody was one of those guys who worked a double last night. He'd fallen on some bad luck and was grateful to get this job building tiny houses. He was driven. Had a goal to save money to buy a new truck. Brad liked the kid. Strong, sinewy build. He was good with his hands, did his job well, and got along with the crew. Cody had even joked he'd get "one of 'em tiny houses" if he had the money.

Brad gritted his teeth. Cody had his dreams. He wanted a truck and a house. He didn't ask for more. He did honest work, a hard day's work to earn his living. But now he was lying on a hospital bed, injured. It'd been an accident, from what he heard. Cody had been working on the ladder when the misstep occurred as he was rushing to finish. It wasn't fair, Brad thought.

Life had flown by. Ten years ago, he had his dreams, like Cody. He'd pursued them in the city, going to college and working in construction to make extra money on the side. After graduation, he continued in the trade and learned everything he could in the business, quickly moving into management. When Brad traveled to another city for a meeting, he saw his first tiny home community. He'd come back excited, inspired, and couldn't get it out of his head. It became his goal, his project. He did research, scouted locations, and put together a business plan and budget. He secured a loan from the bank and then quit his job.

All the hard work had been satisfying and worthwhile. They'd just completed the first tiny house, which would serve as the model home while the others were being built. It was his pride and joy to see this finished home. All five hundred square feet of it.

He sighed as he laid a gentle hand on Cody's arm and stood up. It came at a cost, and Cody paid the price. He couldn't stop the feeling of sadness and guilt as he left the hospital room.

If only he hadn't rushed to complete the model home. If only obstacles hadn't been thrown in the way. If only there hadn't been problems and unexpected barriers. He'd wrestled with every decision. Each of which affected other areas—it was a moving thing with multiple parts. Brad had taken on more than he'd known. But he was determined to finish this project and do the best that he could and not cut corners. Not with materials or workmanship. And he owed his crew, who labored beside him.

It was night when he walked out of the hospital, the automatic sliding doors quietly closing behind him. He stood outside, momentarily forgetting where he parked his car. It had been a stressful day. The night sky was dark, the stars covered by clouds. A wave of loneliness swept over him. He looked up, searching for the moon. And an expanse of blackness as far as he could see met his gaze. There wasn't a bit of moon peeking out on this dark, cloudy night. He shivered and raised his head to the sky once more, as if seeking a change.

Finally, he reached into his pocket for his car keys. He clicked his key fob, listening for the beep. It was eerie and quiet this time of night. His ears made out the faint response to his clicking. He walked in that direction and clicked once more. He heard the chirp again, louder this time. A bit of energy surged through his body, down his legs. He turned toward his car.

30

———

THE BLINDING GLARE OF HEADLIGHTS CAME OUT OF nowhere, swerving as a vehicle sped toward the hospital entrance. Stunned momentarily, Brad froze, one hand clutching his key fob. The screech of rubber over the pavement snapped his gaze as his legs propelled him forward, the lurch destabilizing him, causing him to stumble and fall. He heard a car door opening and shouting, then someone bending over him, calling his name.

"Brad."

He frowned, narrowing his eyes to make out the features on the face in the silhouette. Dazed and shaken up, he thought the voice sounded familiar, but was it... her? Could it be *her*?

"Are you hurt?" This time the voice was louder, almost pleading, with a hint of urgency to it.

He raised his arm, pushing his upper body up from the paved road. He tested his legs and stood up, slightly bent over, turning his body so his back was to the headlights. In this position, he saw her. Recognized her.

"Mary—"

"I'm sorry, I almost ran you over."

He glanced back at the dark sedan, engine still running, the door on the driver's side open. His heart was still pounding over the close call. "What... what are you doing here?"

"Laurie—she called me. Right after you talked to her. She heard you mention 'hospital' and thought you'd been injured. She said it was hard to hear with noise in the background. She couldn't get the details. Heard you say 'surgery.' Then you had to go."

"I had to go because I saw the doctor walk up and needed to talk to him about rushing to do the surgery."

"She was worried about you. She called me."

Mary took a step back and scrutinized Brad, glancing from head to toe.

"You don't look like you just had surgery." Her frown deepened.

"Oh, not me. They rushed Cody for surgery on his foot. He was in a lot of pain," Brad clarified. "He was at the construction site working on a ladder when he fell."

"Was the surgery successful?"

"As far as we know. The doctor said Cody is young and in good physical shape. It'll take weeks to months, at least a couple of months, to heal from his broken ankle. He'll need plenty of rest and to let his body do its work."

"But you… are you hurt?"

"No. What are you doing here?"

"Are you glad to see me?"

"I asked you first."

She shuffled her feet, taking her time to answer. Then she inhaled a big breath and slowly let it out. "Okay, here goes. When Laurie called me, I was worried about you. I haven't heard from you since you left."

"So you decided to see for yourself."

"Yes and no. I did, and because Laurie was also worried about you. She said you were in the hospital."

"Well, you almost ran me over, and I almost had a heart attack twice—the second time when I saw it was you."

"I've answered your question. Now it's your turn. Why haven't you called me?"

Brad was still getting over the shock of seeing her. He gathered his thoughts.

"Why?" He repeated her question back to her to stall for time to formulate a response.

He looked down, and then away. "Look, this is what I didn't want you to do. Have expectations. I thought I made it clear when I left."

"I thought we were friends."

"We crossed that line."

"You mean… when we kissed?" She stared at him, eyes unblinking. Then she cupped her hands on both sides of his face and kissed him again, long and sweet. "Is this what you mean?"

He blinked while his brain tried to process what just happened, vacillating, then he responded and kissed her back. Gently. He'd dreamed of this moment, but he couldn't tell her before. It didn't matter now. She was here. Mary.

He didn't think about the pain in the palms of his hands, scraped as he fell to avoid the careening car. He didn't think about the knee throbbing in pain from the weight of his body hitting the ground. He didn't think about his headache, the weariness, the grumbling belly that betrayed his hunger.

His attention was all on Mary. She looked gorgeous. Better than he'd remembered. Her thick, dark tresses cascaded over her oval face, providing a frame around her flawless skin, big eyes, and perfect lips—not too thin and not too generous. They were on his lips now, warm and inviting and gently probing. His body ached as hunger of a different kind lit a fire in him.

31

A LOUD, ANGRY HONK DISTURBED THE PEACE AND BROKE their embrace. Mary jumped, pulling back from Brad. She heard yelling as someone rolled down the driver's side window of a black Beamer and shouted obscenities in passing.

She nudged Brad toward her car's passenger door. "Get in."

"My car's in the parking lot."

"You're in no condition. I'll drive." Mary crooked her arm and led the way around to the passenger door as Brad leaned into her. She opened it and eased him into her car.

He settled in, pulled out his key fob, and clicked it toward the direction of his car, locking it.

Mary heard the sound. "I'll bring you back later."

She ran around to her open driver's door and jumped in, fingers searching for the seat belt and securing it with a click. She heard the same sound as Brad did his.

"Okay, where to?"

Brad gave the address, and Mary punched it into her GPS, which showed the directions to his place. He sank back into the seat, resting his head on the headrest.

The drive to his place was quiet except for gentle snoring coming from the passenger side. Mary smiled and slipped a quick glance at Brad. His face had softened in the dim light, the frown marks relaxed. She resisted the temptation to run her fingers over his five o'clock shadow. Her heartbeat raced. Brad looked so handsome, and he was sleeping like a baby.

The drive was peaceful. Mary relaxed into her seat and took the opportunity to look out the window. The bright lights of the big city. The tall buildings. She wondered if people were still working from the offices where windows were lit. She heard the nightlife blaring from clubs staying open late, with rowdy crowds and drunken shouts. A lone bus passed by with an "Out of Commission" label on the front, on its way to be housed for the night.

The hospital was in the downtown central area of the city. Dense buildings and built-up city blocks packed the area. It was another thirty minutes before she reached the entrance to the highway, with multiple lanes in both directions. There were numerous exits and signs showing food, lodging, and gas. It took her away from the city, to the outskirts. Here, the buildings were spread out, flatter, with room to breathe. The distance between stoplights was farther apart. The tall, sleek buildings faded from sight, replaced by more greenery. Businesses had parking lots in the front, easily accessible, instead of stacked, multistoried parking garages.

Mary checked the map on the dashboard. It was larger and easier to see at night. She'd also put the address on her cell but hadn't turned it on, as the guiding voice was loud and might wake up Brad. A glance to her right confirmed he was still asleep.

In a few minutes, she pulled up into Brad's driveway, which the map showed was their destination. She braked, put the gear in park, and turned off the engine. She stepped out to look over the house.

The exterior lights were on, and she could make out the lovely façade of the house, painted light gray with crisp white trim, a tidy front porch, and a beautiful solid-wood door. Its design was simple, with clean-cut lines. What a welcoming sight to come home to, she thought. She walked around, opened the passenger door, and shook Brad's shoulder.

"Hey, sleepyhead. Time to wake up."

His eyes were still shut. She tugged his arm, pulling his hand. "We're here.

He murmured something that sounded like, "Leave me alone."

She laughed. "C'mon, let's get you inside."

32

Brad thought he was dreaming, hearing a woman's laugh. It sounded playful, happy. He felt a warm breath of air on his cheek. Someone was tugging his arm. He swatted at it like it was an annoying mosquito. But it wasn't an insect, because he heard his name called.

"Brad."

His eyes popped open. It wasn't a dream. Where was he?

He was sitting in an unfamiliar car. He looked out the windshield and recognized his house, and turning to his right, the woman who was huffing and puffing, about to pull his arm—Mary.

It came back to him. The long day—rising early, guzzling milk and cereal, leaving the house, finishing up the final touches on the tiny house model home, the accident, Cody at the hospital, and Mary's car almost knocking him over in front of the hospital parking lot. He vaguely remembered being driven away, and that was all.

Partially embarrassed and at a loss for words, he mumbled, "Thank you." He got out of the car, closed the door, and walked from the driveway to the walkway leading to the front porch. Brad hesitated, turning to wait for Mary, when he realized she wasn't following him. He chided himself for his lack of manners.

"I'll invite you in if you'd like to see the place."

"Oh, I'd love to," Mary said, bouncing up the steps.

Brad found the key, unlocked the front door, and turned on the living room lights.

"Come in," he said, tossing his keys on the entryway console table. He walked around, flipping on the lights, first in the kitchen, and then the dining room and hallway. "The first room to the right is my office, and then the en suite master bedroom and a second bedroom."

She walked around the living room and circled the white leather sofa and love seat.

"It's so cute," she exclaimed.

"I'm going to get cleaned up. I'm covered with the day's construction grime and gravel burns." He held up the scraped areas of his hands. "Make yourself comfortable," he said. "If you're hungry, help yourself to anything in the refrigerator."

"Do you have tea?" Mary asked, smiling.

He walked to the kitchen and opened a drawer. He rummaged around and snatched up a couple of tea bags, then smiled apologetically. "I've got some Earl Grey here. Afraid that's all I have to offer."

"That's fine. I'll boil some water." She reached for the kettle, filled it with water, and turned the heat on.

"Good." Brad watched for a moment, then moved. "I'm going to grab a quick shower."

"Oh, I need to use the bathroom."

He pointed down the hall. "All the way at the end."

MARY SPLASHED warm water on her face. She leaned forward on the bathroom sink, staring at her reflection in the mirror as she patted her face dry with a plain white towel. Weary eyes stared back at her, faint lines visible if she looked hard enough. She'd forgotten to slip her bottle of eye drops into her purse this morning, in a hurry to get on the road. She applied fresh lipstick and smacked her lips. Using the tips of her pinkies, she patted tiny dabs of lipstick on her cheeks and blended it in to give them more color. Her hair was in place, now held in a ponytail holder. She stepped back and assessed her appearance in the mirror.

Her tired-looking eyes could do with a refresh. She searched her purse for eye shadow to reapply it and realized she'd forgotten to bring it, too. Mary turned on the water and pumped a generous dollop from the soap dispenser, lathered and washed her hands, and then dried them. She picked up the lotion bottle and sniffed, detecting a whiff of lavender floral scent, and squirted a small amount on her hands and rubbed it in.

As she set the lotion back down on the bathroom vanity countertop, she saw a toothbrush holder—with a toothbrush sticking up—and a tube of toothpaste next to it, partially hidden behind the soap and lotion dispensers. Her heart skipped a beat. She blinked rapidly, then again, to clear her eyes. What was she thinking? Brad didn't live alone. She peered closer. Brad had his own bathroom, so whose toothbrush was it? She groaned as her thoughts shot back to an image of the blonde woman at Laurie's wedding with Brad —Kell.

Mary's face dropped, and her shoulders slumped as she leaned on the sink. Her fingers gripped the edge of the washbasin. "No, no," she whispered. How could this be? The euphoria she'd felt earlier crashed.

33

THE LOUD WHISTLE ON THE KETTLE STARTLED HER. MARY dashed to the kitchen and turned off the stove burner. She got out two mugs, plopped a tea bag into one, and poured hot water to steep. It was automatic, having made tea countless times, so she could do it in her sleep. She thought of a few options. One, she'd have tea with Brad when he came out of the shower and then leave. Two, she'd confront him and ask the burning question in her mind. Three, she'd leave now before he was done.

Mary took a cautious sip of her hot tea. Whatever option she took, she'd have her tea first. She would not waste it. She closed her eyes and inhaled the faint scent of the soothing drink. The steam flowed over her face, warming her skin, opening her pores. It relaxed her. Put her in a better mood. It was her ritual at night, to have tea before she went to bed. It helped to calm her mind for a good rest.

She felt her muscles relaxing, the anxiety slipping away. Her nerves quietened.

"How's the tea?"

Mary's eyes flew open at the sound of Brad's voice.

He was standing in front of her in his bare feet, his damp hair tousled and a mess, wearing a T-shirt that had wet spots clinging to his manly chest and a loose pair of lounge or running shorts. He looked like he hadn't towel-dried thoroughly and had been in a hurry to dress.

Her eyes widened, and she felt a flutter in her stomach. She swallowed. Leaving was not an option. Not now. Not when this delicious, fresh-out-of-the-shower hunk of a man was standing above her, grinning like an idiot.

"Oh, I'll get you your tea." She jumped up nervously and went to the kitchen.

"Need help?"

"No, you stay there."

He leaned back on the couch and watched her.

She didn't have to think as her hands made the familiar motions. When the tea bag was in the mug, she brought it back to the couch.

"Watch out, it's hot," she said, setting the mug down on a coaster on the coffee table as his hand reached out to grab it.

Their hands touched. Her heart beat faster. His shoulder bumped hers when they straightened up. She was suddenly aware of how close his body was.

She heard herself giggle. "Oh, excuse me," she murmured.

He leaned forward, his finger lifting the stray hair that had slipped out from her ponytail.

She couldn't take her eyes off him.

He stroked her cheek lightly, then leaned over and whispered in her ear, "You don't need to apologize."

Then he kissed her.

She melted into his kiss. She wrapped her hands around his neck and stroked his hair. Felt the water drops shake loose and drip on her forehead and nose. She laughed, and he joined in.

He reached for a tissue from the box on the table and touched her chin. "Here?"

She squealed. "No."

He dabbed her eyebrow. "And here?"

She nodded.

He slid the tissue down her nose. "How about here?"

She laughed, licking a droplet that landed on her lips, and pulled his head down for another kiss. "Here."

34

———

BRAD TWISTED HIS BODY AND LEANED AGAINST MARY, shifting his weight on the couch. He felt a shift in her, her muscles tensing up.

"Am I hurting you?" He eased back.

"No." She squirmed, sliding her arm from under him and pulling up to a sitting posture. "I need to go."

He paled, caught unprepared and confused. He swallowed hard and made an offer. "You can stay. I have an extra bedroom."

She straightened her clothes and stood up. "I'll be back in the morning to give you a ride back to the hospital."

He frowned. "Are you sure?"

She gathered her stuff and put her coat on. "I'm sure, thanks," she said, softening it with a smile.

Brad walked her to the front door. He opened it slowly, asking, "What time?"

"Nine o'clock."

He watched her as she left, her heels clacking in the night. Maybe she was tired? Maybe she wanted to be alone tonight? With a heavy sigh, he closed the door behind him and turned out the lights.

35

MARY HAD SET HER ALARM FOR EIGHT IN THE MORNING and placed it on the nightstand by the bed. When it rang, she woke up and stared at the unfamiliar, cheesy painting on the wall, the plain dresser, and the TV in the hotel room. It all came back to her. The hospital. Last night. Brad. The kiss.

Mary allowed a bitter smile, remembering the toothbrush in the bathroom. She convinced herself she'd made the right decision. Leaving had been hard, but she remained firm in her resolve.

She dressed quickly in a pullover and dark pants, brushed her teeth, combed her hair, and applied makeup. It was twenty minutes after eight. Plenty of time to make the trip to Brad's house. Mary grabbed a to-go cup of coffee in the hotel lobby, then headed out.

The city looked different in the morning, bustling with people and crowded lanes of vehicles. She rolled down the window halfway, hearing the street noises.

Amid the hum of car motors, people were talking and shouting, horns honked, and buses braked and revved up after stopping, releasing blasts of fumes. She listened to the directions on her phone for her destination.

Mary arrived a few minutes early. Brad's home was a modest house. It looked more charming in the daylight than she remembered from last night. Clean sidewalks, manicured lawn, and a quiet neighborhood. She stayed in her car and texted him. He texted back immediately to say he'd be right out. She sipped her coffee, still warm in the cup. It tasted harsh, strong, and bitter. But it did the job. She didn't feel like eating this morning and had skipped breakfast.

Brad didn't keep her waiting long. He was out the door and at her car in a matter of about a minute. She smiled as he slid into the passenger seat, inhaling a whiff of masculine cologne.

"Sleep well?" he asked.

"Better than I hoped for."

"Where did you go?"

"I rented a hotel room. Nothing fancy."

He let it go at that. "Good."

"So I'll be your chauffeur," she said. "Have you heard from the hospital?"

"I talked to the doctor after rounds this morning. Cody will be discharged later today. It's great news."

"Back to the hospital now?"

"Not yet. I'd like to show you something first." Brad

paused, eyes reaching hers. "The tiny homes. Would you like to see it?"

"Would I? Heck, yes." She clapped her hands with childlike glee.

"Let's go," he said, matching her excitement.

Brad gave directions and Mary drove. "How far is it?"

"About ten minutes."

The road narrowed away from the neighborhood. It was a scenic drive. The weather was gorgeous.

Mary made a turn into the entrance at a sign that said "Tiny Homes Village Farm."

"Go straight to the front, and you'll see the model home," Brad said, pointing to the left.

Mary gawked at the stunning, tiny blue structure as she parked in front of it. "Oh wow, it's so cute!"

Her eyes were wide open like a kid in the candy store; she couldn't take it all in. The new windows glinted and sparkled in the sunlight. A skylight was visible in the roof. Two wooden rocking chairs sat on the front porch, giving a rustic, welcoming feel.

"Can we go in?" she gushed in excitement.

They got out of the car. Brad unlocked the front door and ushered her inside.

"Would you look at that!" Mary said, seeing the gorgeous, bright, and modern interior.

Brad led her on a tour of the full kitchen with stainless-steel appliances, a living room/office combo, a bathroom with a small sink, toilet, and shower, a washer and dryer, and he pointed out cubby holes and creative storage areas.

"That's the first floor."

"There's a loft up there?" she asked, craning her neck.

"Yes, it's a sleeping loft. I'll show you."

He climbed the stairs and stopped at the top. "Watch your head."

She stepped up to the bright loft. "Wow, I love the skylight."

"It brings in a lot of natural light."

"This is cozy. You can lie in bed and read."

"And on rainy days, listen to the pitter-patter." He turned toward the steps. "Ready to go? I'll show you the outside."

"Lead the way."

"Each tiny house has a slightly different look so that no two homes are the same," Brad said. "Another distinction will be the exterior house colors. They will be varied, and you won't see two of the same color next to each other."

Mary nodded. "They'll be unique."

He let her outside and pointed to the homes under various phases of construction. "See these houses? They're in phase one."

"You're planning to expand?"

"Yes, if all goes well, then there's phase two."

"What's in the next phase?"

"More tiny houses, of course. We're starting with a community garden in the first phase and maybe expanding it to add a greenhouse. We're also planning to build a community center with a café and perhaps a small store."

"I like those ideas." She glanced at the site, envisioning Brad's dream—and the future. But there was one person she was dying to ask about. She kept her voice light, casual, and low-key. "I haven't seen Kell around. Is... is she still working for you?"

She held her breath.

He barked a laugh. "Kell? She's long gone. Kell almost broke me, pulling a stunt behind my back. She was ruthless, aggressive, and greedy, and became a competitor who'd do anything to get an edge on a business she was secretly setting up. And that's what she did. Double-crossed me." He shook his head and let out a long breath. "In hindsight, it was a hard lesson. I'd trusted her again, but I learned from it, and in the end, I became a better person, and the business is in a better place."

He touched her hand and tugged. "Come, I have one more thing to show you." He didn't let go of her as he led the way.

Mary was acutely aware of his hand holding hers, the touch and warmth of it. Her heart hammering, she focused on keeping pace with Brad, even as her legs felt weak and wobbly, as he walked ahead. Her eyes fixed on the back of his lean body and strong, sinewy arms.

She felt a closeness to him that words couldn't

describe. And shy, as she embraced the sweet bloom of love.

She focused her attention on him, all of it, and in that moment, she was unaware of her surroundings. When Brad suddenly stopped, she almost ran into him.

He turned to her, beaming.

She gazed into his eyes, seeing what didn't need words.

He nudged her gently. "Look over there."

Ahead, a looming rock monument appeared, rising toward the sky in a clearing surrounded by green space and trees—exactly like the drawing in her school notepad.

Mary blinked and did a double take. Her mouth dropped.

She remembered that day, in the hallway in high school, when she collided with Brad, and her sketchpad fell open to the page with her drawing. The drawing of the rock formation. He'd seen her sketches, her secret art she shared with no one.

"This is yours?" he had asked, picking up her sketchpad.

She had nodded, wordlessly.

"I know this place."

It was stating the obvious. Everyone knew the place. He had glanced down at it again, close up. Scanned the drawing. Would he notice how she'd changed the landscape of the rock formation and added things in the sketch? She'd filled in the spaces where there were bare spots—she'd drawn something there. But she didn't fill it haphazardly, adding random things to the picture. It was careful, thoughtful, and with purpose and meaning.

Had Brad's mind taken a snapshot of it? How else could he have remembered after all these years?

It'd been a surprise when Brad drove her to Craig's Rock near their hometown. The realization hit her now—*why* Brad had taken her to the rock formation. All those years ago, in high school, he'd only briefly glimpsed her drawing pad. But he hadn't forgotten about it—and had built a replica of her sketch here in the city. Brad had discussed with her his project, the Tiny Homes Village Farm, but he'd left out one important thing—the rock monument. In this moment of clarity, surprise turned to joy swelling in her heart, filling and overflowing it.

"You did this for me?" she said. Her eyes brimmed with happy tears and something else—love.

"Yes," Brad said, kissing away her tears before landing a tender kiss on her lips.

36

———

When Brad deepened the kiss, she returned it, stretching her arms up and wrapping them around his neck.

He had spent years nursing his hurt and resentment. He'd been unable to let go and forgive Mary for her actions in high school with the prom and Jim. But it gave him no joy. The more he held on to his bitterness and anger, the more resentful he became.

That day with Mary at Craig's Rock changed everything. Brad changed. It was the first time he felt hope and a ray of brightness entered his outlook, pushing its way through the darkness. He found out what had inspired Mary to draw it on her sketchpad. He experienced it. With her. In that place. In God's country. It had inspired him.

When he'd returned to the city, Brad had sat at his desk and taken out a sheet of paper and a pencil. He worked quickly, making a rough drawing of the rock formation he'd seen in Mary's sketch, refreshed by their visit to Craig's Rock. His hands moved faster and faster, smoothing in the rough areas, pumped by the increased energy flowing to his fingertips. When he was done, he surveyed his work. Satisfied, he sat back in his chair.

It had taken months to build. He oversaw it and got his hands dirty and callused working on it. It was a labor of love. And when it was finished, he knew he'd done everything he could.

This was what mattered. Mary mattered.

"I love you," he whispered, cradling her head in his rough-skinned palm.

EPILOGUE

THAT FIRST TIME BRAD TOOK MARY TO SEE THE TINY Homes Village Farm and the rock monument was a turning point in their relationship. It became their special place. Their safe place to be emotionally vulnerable. That day, they stayed and talked for hours. And cried. And laughed. And talked some more. It was the beginning of many conversations. Honest conversations. Hard conversations. Difficult conversations that had to take place for days.

They rehashed the senior year prom thing and Jim until they were talked out. Brad bared his feelings, and Mary listened. Mary bared her feelings, and Brad listened. It all came out—first the hurt, anger, resentment, bitterness, and disappointment. Between the angst and the bile were the tears: sharp, biting, raw, and bitter-sour tears welled up from deep pools of choked-up reservoirs. And tears of self-pity, betrayal, and long-held grudges. Everything they endured. There were no more secrets, no holding back.

Eventually, their talk turned to the shy childhood crushes, the awkward teenage flirtations, the suppressed desires, and the blossoming of mature love. Sad tears gave way to tears of joy, sighs of happiness, laughter over silly memories, a sense of wonder at being together finally, a sudden shyness, a blush, and the glowing radiance of love.

And they talked about the future. They shared their hopes and dreams, adding brick by brick to a new, firm foundation. Mary worked together with Brad to build the tiny homes village, finding the physical labor hard yet satisfying.

One day, under the soft dusk of a sultry evening by the towering rock monument, they lay in each other's arms and marveled at their happiness at last and the long journey to get there.

That night, back at Brad's house, they took all the time in the world to make love—sweet, tender kisses, gentle caresses, exploring each other's body. As breathing quickened, blood rushed, hearts beat faster, and muscles tensed, long-suppressed urges were aroused and released, filling his once-lonely home with cries of laughter and deep, intense pleasure. They held each other tightly, rested, and started again—giving their hearts and loving—until sunrise, when the rays of sunlight streamed through the sheer bedroom curtains.

They celebrated with laughter and love when the

tiny homes were completed. Cody had recovered by then, and he was the proud owner of a new tiny house with a thirty-year mortgage. And to Mary's delight, she found out he'd come back to get the toothbrush he'd left in Brad's home. He'd sheepishly retrieved it, all the while thanking Brad for letting him crash at his place many nights after working long, exhausting days when he was too tired to drive home.

Jim visited the couple in the city. He delivered his heartfelt apologies for his drunken behavior and thanked Mary and Brad for taking him home and tucking him safely in bed. He was back to his sober and sane self and happier than he'd been since falling into a slump after Katie and Chase's wedding. When he'd served as Chase's best man, it brought up the past, reminders of the good times he had with Mary and the newlyweds. His buried hurt and feelings of rejection and vulnerability had resurfaced, even though the breakup with Mary had been amicable. That drunken incident was a wake-up call, and he'd taken the time he needed to heal.

Katie was thrilled when Mary called her, Chase, and their momma to share her wonderful news. Katie expressed how happy she was for her sister and Brad to be together, and added that she had long gotten over her childhood crush on Brad.

Brad and Mary planned a special ceremony—their wedding—in the Tiny Homes Village Farm. Her momma gave the bride away. Katie and Laurie served as the two matrons of honor. It was an outdoor event with family and friends, in the clearing surrounded by woods in front of the rock monument, which was a replica of the drawing Mary had sketched many years ago, and Brad had brought her dreams to reality. They found their happiness at last.

BY JANE SUEN

Children of the Future

ROMANCE

This Time Around

Reckless Heart

EVE SAWYER MYSTERIES

Murder Creek

Murder at Lolly Beach

Murder off Route 82

FLOWERS IN DECEMBER TRILOGY

Flowers in December

Coming Home

Second Chance

ALTERATIONS TRILOGY

Alterations

Game Changer

Primal Will

SHORT STORIES

Beginnings and Endings: A Selection of Short Stories

I Ain't Afraid of Nothin'

ABOUT THE AUTHOR

Jane Suen is a *USA Today* bestselling author who writes mysteries, sci-fi thrillers, short stories, contemporary romance, and crime fiction.

9 781951 002244